PHANTOMS
CAN BE
MURDER

CONNIE SHELTON

PHANTOMS
CAN BE
MURDER

Charlie Parker Mystery #13

CONNIE SHELTON

Secret Staircase Books

Phantoms Can Be Murder
Published by Secret Staircase Books, an imprint of
Columbine Publishing Group
PO Box 416, Angel Fire, NM 87710

Printed and bound in the United States of America
ISBN 1477496238
ISBN-13 978-1477496237

Book layout and design by Secret Staircase Books
Cover image © Connie Shelton
Cover background image © cekur

First trade paperback edition: May, 2012
First e-book edition: May, 2012

For Dan, always my partner and my inspiration

Chapter 1

The letter arrived on a Tuesday, a pale purple envelope that smelled like a candle shop and bore a British postmark. It slid out of the stack of mail that I'd tossed on the dining table and I debated between ripping it open immediately (curiosity and impatience being two of my stronger suits), or opening all the bills first and then savoring this strange new arrival (saving the best for last). Curiosity won out. The looping backhand script delivered surprising news.

Dearest Charlotte,

I am your aunt Louisa. We have never met. It's a long story, one with some regrets. But retelling the tale isn't the purpose of my letter today. Life has moved on, beyond the judgments and hurts of those earlier times, I would hope. I've certainly been remiss in not contacting you sooner, but I hope we can move along past that.

May I phone you? I would be most interested to know how your life has turned out. I shall attempt a telephone call within the next week.
       Fondly,
         Louisa Charlotte Parker
         Bury Saint Edmunds, Suffolk

I have to admit that my first reaction was to think that Bury Saint Edmunds sounded more like a religious edict than an actual place. My second reaction was to call my brother Ron and demand to know why I'd never heard of this aunt.

"You have too heard of her." His tone went immediately argumentative on me. "You were named for her." He didn't add *Dweeb*, but I heard it.

My thoughts flew. Mother had told me that I was named after *two* maiden aunts—I felt sure that was the story—and I'd always pictured them living about four generations ago, back when hemlines still touched the ground. Why did no one ever tell me these things?

"Dad's sister," Ron continued. "The one he had the falling out with, the one he never spoke to."

"Which explains why *I* never heard of her." I sulked for another two seconds. "She's written to me." I held up the letter, shaking it, as if he might see it over the phone and understand everything.

"What does she say?"

"Something about regrets from years gone by, and that she's going to call me. Other than that, nothing. The whole thing is two paragraphs." I set the page back on the dining table and paced into the kitchen, tugging open the refrigerator door in search of a bottle of water. "So, *what* past regrets is she talking about?"

"How should I know? Mom mentioned Aunt Louise maybe once or twice ever. I was a kid. I never asked. After they died, I got a couple of letters from her, condolence kind of stuff, but I guess I never answered."

That would be *so* like Ron.

"Aunt Louise." My birth-certificate name is Charlotte Louise Parker, so okay, I got that. And I could have been wrong about the story of there being two aunts; I didn't pay attention to a lot of what my mother told me. "She signs this letter Louisa."

I could almost hear Ron's shrug over the phone. "Charlie, what can I say? It's been nearly twenty years since I heard boo from her."

Papers shuffled in the background. "Look, I gotta run. Victoria's waiting for me to meet her at Pedro's for enchiladas."

His newest girlfriend, this time fairly serious.

Since he was providing no help whatsoever, I turned to the better source for family history, my neighbor Elsa Higgins. Our puppy, Freckles, followed on her gangly four-month-old legs through the break in the hedge to Elsa's back porch. The tiny brown and white fluff-ball that we'd adopted back in June had become my shadow and it was unthinkable that I would make it the whole twenty yards to the neighbor's place without her company.

"Well, look at that little one," Elsa exclaimed as the dog bounded into the kitchen and planted herself right in front of the spot where a jar of treats sat on the countertop. "I swear she's three sizes bigger every time I see her."

A guilty twinge reminded me that it had been over a week since my last visit. I really should be checking daily on Elsa. Nearing ninety, still maintaining her lifestyle at home, she's a complete wonder. But still, things can happen and I needed to be more diligent. When I was orphaned at fifteen, she took me in and raised me through surely the most hellacious years of any teenager's life, until I was old enough to move back into the family home next door. As my surrogate grandmother, surely she would know the whole history behind this surprise aunt in England.

She adjusted her glasses and took the letter, settling into a chair at her kitchen table. I raided the cookie jar for myself and the treat jar on behalf of Freckles.

"England . . . well, isn't that something?" she said.

"Elsa! This aunt, Louisa. Who is she?"

"I'd guess she's your father's sister." She looked up at me blankly. "Well, the last name being Parker and all."

"You never heard anyone in my family mention her?"

"Well, honey, your folks moved in next door when Ron was a toddler. Paul came along very shortly, then you a few years later. I never knew much about their lives before that. Your mother was always busy with you kids, her gardening and the country club set, and your dad worked such long hours and all." She rubbed at a place on the back of her neck. "Louisa . . . let me think . . ."

I knew better than to rush the process. It was a little like watching grass grow. However, for all her years, Elsa does not have one single withered brain cell so this wasn't a matter of her simply forgetting. She genuinely didn't know. I sank down into the chair across the table from her.

"She says she'll call. When she does, just ask her."

Well, that was just way too simple. I gave Elsa a hug and trekked back to our side of the hedge, putting the aunt out of my mind as I tried to decide what to make for dinner when Drake got home.

Of the two of us, my wonderful hubby is actually the better cook and I often defer to his expertise. While he takes fresh things from the fridge and chops, dices and tosses them into a pan to come up with the most wonderful meals, I lean more toward opening a package of this and a can of that. I *am* quite adept with the buttons on the microwave. But, in this instance, I'd put in a short day at the office of the private investigation firm I co-own with my brother, while Drake had been flying all day, scouting film locations with what had probably been a pain-in-the-something Hollywood movie producer. I couldn't very well ask him to make dinner on top of all that. So I leaned into the freezer and found one of those fifteen-minutes-in-a-skillet dinners, then set to work making a salad to go with it.

By the time he walked in the door I had a good-sized batch of chicken, veggies and pasta bubbling away in a yummy sauce.

"Something sure smells good in here," he said, nuzzling my neck as he slipped his arms around me.

Whether he was referring to the dinner or to my cologne, either was preferable to the eau de jet fuel that emanated from his flight suit. I suggested that I could keep the meal warm while he grabbed a quick shower. Luckily, he took the hint and emerged ten minutes later from the bathroom in a considerably more desirable state.

Although we will celebrate our third anniversary in a little over a month, people tease us about acting like honeymooners. Catching a whiff of Drake's fresh clean skin and seeing the way the ends of his damp hair curled around his ears . . . well, I turned off the burner on the stove and undid the buttons on his shirt way faster than he'd buttoned them.

The packaged meal wasn't in great shape—congealed sauce over limp vegetables—when we emerged from the bedroom an hour later. I dumped the lumpy mess while Drake adeptly sliced some cheese and an apple, and we took the impromptu feast with two glasses of wine back to the bedroom where we leaned against stacks of pillows and put a comedy movie in the DVD player. Freckles whimpered a little at the smell of the food but soon gave up and went to her bed in the corner. I felt my eyelids grow heavy and I guess I blinked out before the movie was even halfway done because the next thing I knew I was waking to the sound of Drake's alarm and his groan at having to report back to another day of flying that movie producer around in his helicopter.

He was in the shower and I'd just nestled the comforter around my shoulders when the telephone rang.

"Charlotte? Is that you? I hope I've figured the time correctly and it isn't the middle of the night there or anything."

Not quite. My bedside clock said 6:24. As this could only be Aunt Louisa I took a deep breath, worked up a chipper tone, and hoped I didn't sound entirely incoherent as I welcomed this stranger into my life.

"Oh, lovely. I'm so relieved that you kept your parents' phone number. Charlotte, you can't possibly know how much I've anticipated this day."

I wished I could say the same, but I'd had hardly any notice so I focused my efforts on what I do when I find myself investigating a new situation—paying attention to details. The accent was interesting, essentially American peppered with English phrases and a hint of some other Euro-speak. I had a harder time pegging her age. By the time she'd covered the fact that she was, indeed, my father's sister, younger by twenty years, and had lived in England for quite some time, I'd awakened sufficiently to pose a few questions.

"I spoke with my brother Ron yesterday after your letter came. He sounded apologetic that he'd never responded to your earlier correspondence. I hope you won't think we're all as lacking in manners."

"Not at all, dear. I just wasn't sure whether you would welcome my call. Perhaps your father had influenced your opinions toward me in some way . . ."

"He actually never mentioned you at all. I'm sorry. I don't know what the rift was about. I didn't even know you existed."

There was a brief silence on the line. "I was afraid of that. Bill was so absolutely set in his ways. The kind of man who, once he'd formed an opinion, would not let go of it. At least as far as people were concerned. I can only assume he was more open to ideas in his scientific field."

I couldn't answer that question either. Until recent years I'd known nothing at all of my father's top secret work during the cold war years. Even after an investigation three years ago into his death, precious few details of his actual projects had emerged.

"At any rate, I want to know you better. I haven't much money for travel, but would absolutely adore it if I could host you here sometime."

Drake walked out of the bathroom, sending a quizzical look my direction as he proceeded to dress. I made my excuses to Louisa and promised we would speak again soon.

"What on earth was that about?" he asked as I slipped into my thick fuzzy robe and headed toward the kitchen to start the coffee.

I filled him in on the call and he perused the letter while I buttered bread and stuck it into the toaster oven.

"Ron remembers her, barely. I've never met her, but now she wants us to come for a visit."

"Is she for real?" he asked, spreading strawberry jam on his toast.

"Luckily, I have the means of finding that out. Background checks are our specialty."

He left for the final day of his film recon job, and Freckles and I headed for the offices of RJP Investigations a little while later. By the end of the day Ron and I had come up with sufficient background on Louise Charlotte Parker—who had legally changed her name to Louisa more than thirty years ago—that I felt comfortable in knowing that I truly did have an aunt who lived in England.

Several more phone calls over the ensuing days told me a lot more about the who, just not much about the why. Why had she picked this time to contact me? Why had she and my father not spoken since I was born?

Ron, with an investigator's natural skepticism, cautioned me to watch for ulterior motives. "She may be looking for someone to pull her out of some financial bind," he said. I chalked the attitude up to his own experiences with his ex-wife because we hadn't found anything of that nature in the background checks on Louisa.

"She keeps repeating the invitation to come see her," I told Drake one evening over green chile chicken enchiladas at Pedro's, our favorite little hole-in-the-wall restaurant.

Louisa and I had now spoken over the phone a half-dozen times. "What do you think? Want to go?"

He reached over and took my hand, giving it a squeeze. "It started out as a pretty rough summer, babe. Maybe a break would be good for you. Change of scenery couldn't hurt."

He referred to the fact that in June I'd been held hostage for several days by a gang of desperate men. And even though they'd all been caught, I still woke with nightmares, three months later, and I hadn't yet gotten comfortable working late in my office the way I used to do.

I booked our reservations that night and found a boarding kennel for Freckles, figuring that a puppy was a bit much for Elsa to handle, and it looked like we were on our way to London. I'd decided to break into the bank account and splurge on business class tickets, in keeping with Drake's idea that this vacation should be a totally relaxing experience for me. It would have all been perfect, but for the last-minute phone call three days before the trip in which one of his steady clients needed helicopter work done and threatened to take all his business elsewhere if Drake couldn't handle the job.

"Hon, I have no choice," he said. "I cannot afford to turn this down. You go without me."

I'd already squeezed the trip in between two other important commitments and there would be no foreseeable chance to reschedule for many months. I'd psyched myself up for the trip, based on Louisa's descriptions of her charming town, and I'd worked like a demon to clear my calendar at work.

Drake watched the conflicting emotions flicker across

my face. "Do it. You girls will have a much better time without me anyway."

I doubted that, but since his work frequently took him away for days, sometimes weeks, at a time I didn't feel entirely guilty about taking this little jaunt purely for myself. And so that's how I found myself in a jumbo jet over England, hearing the pilot's announcement that we would soon be landing at Heathrow.

Chapter 2

Louisa had insisted on picking me up at the airport and driving me to Bury St. Edmunds herself. As she explained it, the trains could get a little tricky if you'd never been there before. I appreciated that plus I thought the two hour car ride would give us the chance to get to know each other better.

Clearing customs and toting my awkwardly weighty bag behind me, I spotted her amid the ranks of drivers holding up corporate placards for my fellow passengers. I recognized her face from photos she'd emailed me. In return I'd emailed her a few shots of Drake and myself but forewarned her that I would be traveling alone. She spotted me in the crowd and we edged toward each other.

"You're tall like your dad," she said as we broke from a quick embrace.

At five-seven I'm not exactly towering, but my aunt was

several inches shorter, with wispy shoulder-length blond hair, a pear-shaped body, dressed in layers of floaty fabrics in shades of purple and turquoise. Her smile was bright and genuine and her blue eyes sparkled happily when she spoke.

"We're over here," Louisa said, gesturing toward a parking area across a few lanes of traffic. She insisted upon taking the handle of my suitcase. The bag and I trailed along in her wake at a quick pace.

Through my fog from a long plane trip with little sleep, despite the stretch-out accommodations in business class, I followed her to the parking garage looking for any resemblance between her and my father. Dad had been tall, straight and serious, with the receding hairline that Ron inherited and the almost-formal demeanor that he'd acquired as a doctor of science. His genetics were nowhere to be seen in Louisa. The closest I could compare was to my brother Paul, who has the same coloring and is slighter in build than Dad or Ron.

Louisa moved like a small sprite, turning her head to check the traffic, heading into the crosswalk with her swift steps, glancing over her shoulder to be sure I was with her. By the time I'd figured out that she was aiming for a small blue Ford and I'd incorrectly headed for the wrong side of it, she'd popped open the trunk and hefted the suitcase into it as if it were nothing.

"There now," she said with a laugh. "I think we're good to go."

I settled into the left-hand front seat as she backed out and negotiated a completely confusing maze of lanes and corners to take us out of the airport. The tires chirped as she reached the on-ramp of some major thoroughfare.

"Have you visited the UK before?" she asked, once we'd joined the flow of traffic.

I reoriented myself to the fact that cars coming at us on the right was an okay thing, and told her a little about the helicopter job Drake and I had taken in Scotland a couple years ago. Aside from a quick pass through London on our way to Inverness, this was my first time in England.

By the time we reached the outskirts of St. Edmundsbury township I'd learned that the town was named for King Edmund, martyred in 869 AD, and that it had been a thriving marketplace well before then. That Louisa was younger than my father by twenty years, that she'd legally changed the spelling of her first name after a trip to Italy and a romance with a charmer, and that the rolling fields we passed contained maize and sugar beets. Her narrative was as erratic as her driving, but at least it was informative. I still didn't quite find out what had caused the rift between the siblings but I was determined to learn that soon.

We passed the sugar factory, which I recognized immediately by the sticky-sweet smell that I remembered from similar facilities in Hawaii where I'd met Drake. The streets narrowed as we reached the older section of town, with an eclectic mixture of stone and brick buildings whose doorways opened directly onto the narrow sidewalks. A medieval arch appeared on our left.

"The Abbey Gate," Louisa explained. "This part of the town has been inhabited since the Middle Ages. We'll take a walk through the Abbey Gardens in a bit, if you're up to it."

A walk sounded like the perfect antidote to the long hours confined in airplane and car, and I readily agreed to the plan.

"This is the Angel, here on the right," she said. "Are you sure you won't change your mind and stay at my house?"

The Angel Hotel, where I'd made reservations, had operated in its present location since 1452, an imposing three stories of gray-brown stone completely covered in ivy with lush purple petunias sprouting from planters beneath each window. When the plan was for Drake to travel with me, it only seemed sensible to stay in a hotel rather than impose on my aunt's hospitality. Her offer was tempting but seeing the historic building kind of took my breath away. I needed to experience this at least once.

Louisa sensed my hesitation and pulled into the parking area in front of the hotel. "Here we are, then."

"I really appreciate your offer," I said. "They would have charged my account for at least one night anyway—"

"Charlie, it's absolutely not a problem," she said, switching off the ignition and turning toward me. "You will love this place. And if you spend a night or two and want to switch, I'm sure they can accommodate the change. My home is only about a ten minute walk from here, and I work at the tourism office just that way—" She waved vaguely toward the next block. "You can find me whenever you want."

We stepped out of the car and met at the back where she reached for my bag in 'the boot.' "Besides," she said with a twinkle in her eye, "if you're here at the Angel you might get a chance to see one of the ghosts."

Ghosts? Sure.

I might as well admit right now that I'm a supreme cynic about that stuff. Not one supposedly haunted old house or hotel or graveyard that I've ever visited has shown me any evidence whatsoever of the famed supernatural residents.

Louisa, on the other hand, had told me during the long drive that she studied astrology and ancient folk legends in college—hinting that this curriculum may have led, in part, to the rift with my ultra scientific father. I could vouch for his distrust of the unproven—every childhood alibi I tried to construct met with the strictest of testing before he accepted it.

She registered the skepticism on my face. "The Angel Hotel," she said, adopting an official tone, "is reputed to be home of not one, but two, ghosts. One is said to be the fiddler who was sent into the tunnel connecting Angel Hill to a pub in Eastgate Street. The man entered, playing his fiddle so onlookers could track his progress, but he never came out. Modern day spirit activity still seems to center around the cellars of the hotel near the now-bricked up entrance to the tunnel."

She grinned at me. "My job these days is to give tours of 'Haunted Bury St. Edmunds' through the tourism office." She switched back to her tour-guide voice. "Of course, those fortunate enough to stay in the Charles Dickens Room often report odd noises in the night and strange little episodes where items go missing from the room."

"Well, I don't think I'm in the Dickens room," I assured her. "But I'll try not to disturb any of the old residents."

A uniformed bellman appeared just then, rushing down the front steps of the hotel and approaching the car to ask if I was checking in. He hefted my suitcase and headed indoors with it.

"Take a moment to settle in," Louisa suggested. "I'll check in at my office and come back for you. Then we can find some lunch and take that walk around the gardens."

We parted with a quick hug and a plan to meet in thirty

minutes. I trailed the bellman into the lobby which consisted of a series of cozy, low-ceilinged rooms, the central one featuring a wide rock fireplace flanked by large overstuffed couches. I completed the check-in paperwork at a reception desk of dark wood and was directed to follow the bellman— a lengthy trek up a flight of stairs, around a series of sharp turns, along a squeaky corridor which included two steps up and two steps down for no readily apparent reason, a few more turns until we came to a hallway with numbered rooms on the right hand side only. He cheerfully unlocked the door for me and placed my baggage on the floor.

I'd reached for my wallet in hopes of figuring out the strange bills I'd exchanged at the airport when the man cheerfully bade me goodbye and disappeared out the door. No hand fidgeting for a tip? Now that was something you never saw in the States.

It was a good-sized room with a desk in one corner, an antique wooden wardrobe offset by the modern touch of a flat-screen television mounted on the wall beside it, a small round table with full tea service that included electric kettle, a choice of black tea or Earl Grey or coffee, along with every desired sweetener and creamer, plus two packets of cookies. I was loving England already!

The large bed was made up for two—a twinge—how nice it would have been for Drake to be here with me. It was pre-dawn back home so I called Drake's cell, left him a quick message that all was well and suggested that he give me a call once he woke up. A quick brush through my hair and a retouch of lipstick. Short of a six hour nap there wasn't much else I could think to do to myself at the moment. I straightened my jeans and put a wool jacket on over my wrinkled T-shirt and hoped we weren't going anyplace dressy.

Louisa sat tucked into a corner of one of the deep sofas in the lobby when I descended the stairs, miraculously having found my way back along the convoluted tangle of hallways and steps. She tapped a few buttons on her phone and dropped it into her purse.

"There now. Texted my supervisor and I've got the whole afternoon free," she said, practically bouncing up from the couch. "Would you like a sit-down pub lunch or something we can carry to the gardens while we walk around?"

Walking, definitely. She led me out the front of the hotel and we strolled past a dress shop and a place called the Really Rather Good Coffee House. Seriously. I looked twice and smiled at the sign.

The September air felt crisp with a chill on this half-cloudy day. Abbeygate Street was closed to car traffic but the pedestrians were out in force—young mothers pushing strollers, sturdy older women with mesh shopping bags, businessmen who looked barely out of high school striding between the slower groups.

"I grab lunch at this shop at least twice a week," Louisa said, steering me toward a brick building where large windows showed rows of baked items. "Cornish pasties. Like pie crust wrapped around various meats, potatoes, veggies, warm gravy."

The scent coming from the shop was pure meaty, saucy heaven and I felt myself practically begin to drool as I stared at the rows of pastry packets on display. Louisa turned to me from the doorway with a question in her eyes.

"Whatever you normally have," I said, still processing

the sights and smells, never mind deciphering whatever quick question the man behind the counter had posed to us.

"Two, traditional, take away, please," Louisa said. She thrust forward a bill with red printing on it and got some coins back in change.

The warm paper envelope with its treasure of hot meat pie felt good in my hands. If I hadn't been a little faint from hunger I could have held it in my chilly fingers and taken pleasure from that simple act. As it was, by the time we hit the street again we were both unfolding the paper and picking off bits of the flaky pastry and sneaking them into our mouths. The steam that emerged brought back memories of Sunday roast beef-and-potato dinners at Elsa's. I think I moaned at my first real bite of it.

"Yummy, isn't it?" Louisa said. "The chicken and mushroom one is another of my favorites." She had folded her paper packet closed, saving the treat until we could settle somewhere.

We strolled back the way we'd come, emerging from Abbeygate Street and crossing the parking area in front of the hotel. Two-way traffic on Angel Hill Road gave us a moment to pause and stare up at the elaborate stone gate leading to the Abbey grounds. Louisa gave some details of the history of the ancient abbey and the current, more modern one which had received its finishing touches in very recent times. At a glance, I would have never guessed the construction of the elaborate building was completed over more than a thousand years; it all blended seamlessly.

"I'll tell you more of it, if you're interested, another day. You seem to be a little overwhelmed at the moment." She smiled at me with a cheerful sparkle in her eye.

I nodded. "Long trip. By tomorrow I'll be as energetic as ever."

We'd crossed the road and walked under the high arch of the stone gate and the gardens spread out before us. Coming from a high-desert region where cactus are considered ornamental plants and lush greenery is a city park that actually has both grass and trees, I'd had few experiences to compare with a formal English garden. Walkways quartered the open space and in each quadrant closely clipped lawns formed the backdrop for precise plantings of bright flowers in patterns of purple, yellow, pink and red. Benches lined the walks and we found an empty one.

Unwrapping our portable lunch again we savored the scrumptious meat and potato combination. A white-haired gentleman in a three-piece suit gave a sidelong glance. Americans and their informality, his expression seemed to say. About three minutes later, two ducks found us. They each accepted a crumb of our crusts before they politely moved on to solicit the charity of someone else.

"I don't want to tire you too much on your first day," Louisa said, "but there's so much I want to show you. I'm sad that you could only be here for a week."

With no idea what I was getting into I hadn't wanted to commit too much. Now, without Drake's schedule pressing us, I probably could manage to stay longer if things worked out. For now, we would just see how the visit went.

"So, I'm sure you'd like a bit of a rest this afternoon," she was saying. "If you don't mind my popping by the knit shop on the way back, I'll pick up a little more wool for a project I'm working on. I belong to a little weekly knitting group there. Then later, we can have dinner at my house."

"I'm getting my strength back now, I think. Whatever

you've planned sounds good to me." There were at least a dozen questions on my mind, mainly about family and why her relationship with my father had gone so far south. We'd barely touched on the past yet, focusing mainly on our present-day lives during our few brief phone conversations, but I didn't intend to leave England before I knew more about this mysterious new relative of mine.

"Explore around here anytime during your stay," Louisa was saying. "The Abbey grounds are extensive, farther in you'll find the ruins of the oldest sections that date back to the Middle Ages. I've also requested a flexible work schedule this week so we can spend more time together, and it would be a joy to show you all around."

We'd finished our pasties by this time and tossed the wrappers into a discreet trash barrel on the way back out to the street. Heading west on Abbeygate Street, I followed Louisa's lead through several turns into progressively narrower lanes until she abruptly stopped on a picturesque street called Lilac Lane and opened the door to a tiny shop.

"The Knit & Purl" was painted in gold on a carved wooden sign depicting a set of knitting needles thrust through a ball of purple yarn, which hung above the doorway at a ninety-degree angle to the sidewalk. Tiny bells tinkled as the door closed behind us.

A thin woman with angular features and steel-gray hair in a straight page cut looked up from the sales counter. Her body seemed all planes and angles, from the minimal chest to her sharp shoulders and spider-like fingers. She wore navy trousers and a print blouse with a cardigan of blue wool that looked like her own creation. Her face softened when she saw my aunt.

"Ah, Louisa, there you are! I'm so glad you've come."

"Well, I said I'd be by today for the blue heather. Did it come in?" Louisa stopped in mid-stride. "Oh, where are my manners? I want you to meet my niece from the States." She reached out to shuffle me to the forefront.

"Charlie, this is my dear friend, Dolly Jones. She owns this lovely shop. It's only been here a year or so, right Dolly? But hasn't she done a beautiful job with it?"

Dolly regarded me with suspicion for a moment, her light blue eyes squinted nearly shut. "Charlie? Unusual name."

Louisa went into the whole explanation of how I'd been named for her and I added that my brothers had shortened Charlotte to Charlie when we were kids. Dolly's smile brightened, as if now that she knew something about me I had passed muster.

I returned the smile and began to browse the shop when their conversation turned back to the subject of Louisa's blue heather yarn which, it so happened, had not yet arrived. In addition to two walls full of specially constructed bins filled with precise balls of yarn arranged by color, the shop sold candles, cards, and some handmade cloth purses and bags. A shelf near the register held small bottles of essential oils and herbs. One of the cloth purses caught my eye as a possible gift to take home for Elsa and I'd walked over to get a closer look, half listening to the scraps of their conversation I could catch above the soft classical music that played in the background.

"And what about that incident last week? Did you ever find out what was behind that?" Louisa was asking.

"No. And now there's been another." Dolly's voice seemed strained as she straightened some cards in their display rack.

"You know," Louisa said, "people say many buildings in this part of town are haunted."

I moved from the purses to the candles, eavesdropping shamelessly now.

"It was *not* the work of a ghost," Dolly declared in a tone that permitted no argument. "No offense, Louisa, but you know that I don't believe in those things."

Louisa only looked momentarily chastened.

"I spent the entire morning putting the wools back in order. You know how I keep my shop, neat as a pin. The yarns are always arranged by color—the reds, the oranges, the yellows, and so forth." She waved a hand toward the bins of perfectly stacked skeins.

"Oh, I know you do," Louisa murmured. "Neat as a pin, Charlie."

I nodded and stepped over to the sales counter.

Dolly kept talking. "This morning I came down to find everything a complete hodgepodge. All the colors mixed together, the dye lots intermingled, the *merino* was in with the *cashmere* for god's sake!"

Her face had grown very pink. She blew out a breath and turned toward me. "It took Gabrielle and me the entire morning to sort it all out. Gabrielle Tukson is my shop assistant."

"Dolly and Archie live right above," Louisa said, pointing toward the ceiling.

"A small apartment comes with the lease," Dolly added. "Not my husband's first choice but—" She waved the rest of the thought away vaguely.

"So someone came in during the night, while you were right upstairs?" I asked.

Dolly shook her head. "I simply don't see how. I am not a heavy sleeper. And Archie was right in bed beside me the whole night. We never heard a sound. The door bells alone would have wakened me, to say nothing of someone moving about throughout the place."

Louisa raised an eyebrow toward me. "And there was the incident last week . . ."

"Muddy footprints across my shining wood floor. This room was spotless when we turned in the night before. I come down to open shop in the morning and there are large boot prints from the front door, over to the register. But, they didn't lead back outside. Just stopped. Practically right on this spot." She pointed toward the floor at her feet.

"Sounds like a poltergeist to me," Louisa said knowledgeably. "They tend to play tricks, move things around but not do real harm."

Dolly squirmed to remain quiet. I got the feeling that she didn't want to alienate a good customer and friend but she didn't for a minute believe that there was a supernatural cause to the mischief in her shop. She brought the subject back around to Louisa's yarn order and assured her that it should arrive in the Tuesday shipment.

We'd turned to leave and were met at the door by a man.

"Archie," Louisa greeted. "Good to see you again." She performed a quick introduction to Dolly's husband.

I registered a man in his sixties who'd once been tall and slender. Now his shoulders were hunched and he decidedly favored his left hip when he walked. His long, thin face was smooth-shaven with crevices along both sides of his mouth.

He raised his cap, revealing a head of thick gray hair, and gave a pleasant smile and fluttered his long fingers toward us as we said goodbye.

Chapter 3

The scattered clouds earlier in the day had thickened and lowered, giving the streets a shadowy feel and the possibility of rain seemed very real now. We hurried past shops that were clearing—a bookstore, a clothing store featuring woolens from Scotland, a coffee shop, a newsstand—as shoppers picked up the pace, finishing their purchases and heading toward home. In minutes we found ourselves at the front steps of the Angel Hotel again.

My jet-lag was catching up to me. I made a halfhearted offer to have Louisa come up to my room for tea and wasn't terribly disappointed when she suggested that I take a little rest and then come to her house for drinks and dinner. She sketched me a little map on the back of an envelope, assuring me that it was a ten minute walk if it wasn't raining. And if it was, I was to give her a call and she would pick me up.

The phone rang on the nightstand as I entered my room.

"Hi, hon." Drake's voice came over the trans-Atlantic miles as if he were in the next room. I wished that he were.

I filled him in on the flight and the ride to Bury and the day's events.

"Sounds like you could use a nap," he said after the third time I yawned. He assured me that all was going well with his job. I tried to get it straight that he'd flown for the customer while I was on the plane then slept while I was walking around town with Louisa. It was early morning at home and he was ready to head for his helicopter once again. Freckles was doing fine. We were training her to stay in her crate whenever she was home alone, and that seemed to be going well. By the time he got through all the details I'd peeled off my jeans and crawled under the duvet on the bed. My eyes slammed shut at approximately the same time I set the phone receiver back in its cradle.

Thank goodness I'd stopped at the front desk and asked them to give a wake-up call at five o'clock or I would have probably slept the entire night away. When the bedside phone chirped its strange foreign tone I jolted awake, heart pounding, head disoriented.

I took a few minutes to really unpack my bag and hang things in the wardrobe, choosing a fresh pair of jeans and a sweater that wasn't terribly wrinkled. A glance out the window showed the courtyard below to be thoroughly damp but no raindrops dotted the few puddles. The sky seemed to be clearing in the early twilight. I set my seldom-used umbrella beside my purse.

The hot shower and shampoo felt wonderful and I gave

myself over to the whole routine. Even though it would be useless to hope my hair wouldn't fluff uncontrollably in this humidity, I spent time with the curling iron and some kind of styling gunk that was supposed to tame frizz. We would see about that.

Forty-five minutes later, standing on the steps of the Angel, I studied Louisa's map. She'd used street names but two blocks into the stroll, I was still having a hard time spotting them, so I relied mostly on her notes about landmarks. Turn right at the pharmacy and go until you get to the theatre. From there two blocks to the right and the fourth door on the left would be a red one, number 15. I used the brass knocker, mainly because one never got to do that at home.

Louisa answered, wearing a flowered silk dress in shades of blue with a white apron over it and turquoise ballet flats. Her hair touched her shoulders in soft curls of the wash and wear variety. I could imagine her as a teenager with a daisy tucked behind one ear.

"Come in, darling." She'd stowed my umbrella and wool blazer before I knew it. A waft of incense reminded me of the letter I'd received at home.

"Wine?" she offered.

From the brightness in her eyes I guessed that she might have already started. The first floor of the row house seemed to consist of a living room and kitchen. Stairs rose to the left of the front door. I followed her into the kitchen and accepted the glass of cabernet that she poured.

"Afraid I don't do fancy when it comes to food," she said. "It's going to be a simple chicken and veggie casserole and a light salad."

"Sounds perfect."

"While it bakes, let me show you around." She stood in place and spread her hands. "Kitchen. Very simple."

It wasn't a large room but seemed equipped with the necessities—smaller versions of stove and fridge than would be typical in America, but certainly adequate. A countertop in green linoleum, the ubiquitous electric kettle, a table set for two.

We walked through the doorway back to the living room—which Louisa called the parlor—where I'd barely registered the décor as dating back to the 1950s with sturdy upholstered sofa and armchair, a piecrust-style coffee table and matching end table. A small lamp there, a floor lamp at the opposite end of the sofa. A quality rug, a bit worn at the edges, on the polished wood floor. If I'd guessed at Louisa's choice in furnishings based on her dress and manner, this would not have been it, but when she explained that she'd been hired as caregiver to an elderly woman when she first moved to Bury and that the lady had later willed the home to her it all made perfect sense.

I noticed her own touches. An arrangement of candles on the coffee table, photos in silver frames. Two of them showed Louisa—fresh-faced, young, with a group of friends in backpacking gear.

"Just never bothered to shop for new furniture," she said. "This is comfortable. Why throw it out?"

She led the way up the stairs and pointed out the two bedrooms separated by a small bathroom, all facing a tiny landing. Again, the '50s styling, although she'd obviously upgraded the mattresses and bedding, opting for thick comforters and piles of pillows to snuggle into.

"If you should change your mind about the hotel, dear, this one would be yours," she said as we left the guest room with its yellow floral wallpaper and bright royal blue accents.

The timer on the oven saved me from having to answer at that moment as Louisa rushed downstairs. I followed a little behind her, loving the charm of the old house but wanting a few more answers before committing. I still didn't know the full story of why Louisa and my father had not spoken for the last twenty years of his life.

The rich scent of chicken in a creamy sauce filled the kitchen. We took seats at the table and served ourselves from the casserole and the bowl of bright green salad.

Conversation soon turned back to the knit shop and Louisa's friend Dolly.

"I've known her for a few years now. We met through a knitting club here in town. Back when I was the live-in for Mrs. Whitmere I needed something to occupy me during the long hours she slept so I took up needlework. When Dolly opened her own shop, she started a small knitting group there."

"I noticed the beautiful afghans in the bedrooms."

"Dolly and I, we're about the same age, had those types of lives that are so similar in ways and so very different in others. She married, was a homemaker for years, successful husband. I never married, couple of close calls on that, but it always seemed more fun to explore the world. While Dolly found a home career, knitting sweaters for the Scottish wool companies, I zipped around Europe with a rail pass and backpack. No children to raise, for either of us, so we had the free time to pursue hobbies. That shared interest formed the basis for our friendship. She can be a prickly person, though, and I suppose she doesn't have a lot of friends."

She wouldn't be easy as an employer either. I remembered

how worked up she'd become over her yarn stock being out of place. I thought of Louisa's ideas about the unexplained incidents in Dolly's shop.

"You seem to have a difference of opinion about the supernatural," I said as we cleared the table.

Louisa set the dishes into the sink, ran some water over them and poured us each another glass of wine. "Let's relax in the parlor. I guess you could say that I've seen enough not to be a disbeliever, while Dolly has never seen enough to be a believer." She laughed heartily, a sound that filled the small room where we settled at opposite ends of the sofa.

"Let me show you something," she said, setting her wine glass aside and rising to cross to the bookshelves. She pulled out a book with an ethereal pattern of gray smoke on its cover and blew a whiff of dust off the top.

I caught sight of the title—*The World's Top Ten Haunted Sites*.

"This isn't an authority on the subject," she said. "More of a starter volume. I've actually visited all ten of them."

She tucked a wisp of hair behind her ear and opened the book as she settled back onto the sofa.

"In fact, here's one that's very close to home."

I immediately thought of New Mexico, but saw that the heading on the page said *England—Suffolk*. Silly me. The photo at the center of the spread looked a little familiar.

"It's our Abbey," Louisa said. "Right here in Bury."

Now I knew where I'd seen those spires.

"Of course, many of what they consider the 'most haunted' sites in the world center around battlefields and such, places where hundreds or thousands of people have died. What makes our Abbey unique is that it's been inhabited for well over a thousand years and there have been consistent sightings of those from the spirit world during all that time."

I stared at the images, taken in foggy light—the lumpy ruins of the ancient structures alongside the more modern Gothic styled ones that looked like something right out of a 1930s movie set. Or maybe it was the shots of the gravestones tilted at odd angles in the nearby churchyard which gave that impression. Being a sucker for old Hitchcock films and remembering gripping my brother's arm in the theater when he dragged me to a slasher movie without my mother's knowledge, I felt a stirring of interest. Sometime while I was here I would have to visit those old ruins and see if I picked up my aunt's enthusiasm.

Meanwhile, I caught myself stifling a huge yawn. Louisa noticed too.

"It's been a long day for you," she said. "Are you sure you don't want to change your mind and stay here?"

For about half a second I was torn. Her guest room was lovely. But then, my room at the Angel was also lovely. And it would feel good to have a night completely to myself. I made polite noises about the kindness of her offer as I carried my wine glass to the kitchen and looked around for my blazer and umbrella. We parted with a hug.

A light drizzle had begun sometime during the evening but at the moment it had subsided into an atmosphere of dense, cool moisture that didn't actually include any real raindrops. I kept my umbrella folded and let my skin soak it in, understanding how English women got their dewy complexions.

The night streets lay in quiet shadows before me, the

residents of the tiny neighborhood tucked in behind softly glowing windows. Victorian styled street lamps gave just enough light to keep me from becoming completed spooked as my footsteps echoed on the sidewalks. Following Louisa's directions in reverse got me back to the Angel, a little chilled but unharmed by anything of a phantom nature and more than ready to heat the kettle and have a relaxing cup of tea.

Snuggled into my flannel jammies, I only made it halfway through the tea before my eyelids refused to stay open. The thick duvet felt so good as I pulled it up to my chin and I'm pretty sure I was unconscious moments after the lamp went out.

Chapter 4

Sunlight brightened the windows that faced the front of the hotel. It was my first clue that I was in an east-facing room. I stretched and savored the warmth of the covers, up to the moment it became evident that my bladder wasn't going to let me stay in bed much longer. Back from my quick trip to the bathroom I parted the sheer curtain and looked out.

A flurry of traffic moved through the lot, mainly young mothers releasing uniformed kids to begin their day. I hadn't realized there was a school nearby. I pressed the button on the coffee maker, remembering that breakfast was included in my room price but not quite having the energy to get dressed just yet. From the glimpse I'd caught of the restaurant with its high ceilings and dark woods, I had the feeling this wasn't one of those places where you should show up in sweats with your hair in sleep-tangles.

Voices drifted upward, excited kids meeting their friends and heading for class, while I sipped at my coffee and thought about the past few days. Louisa with her bright smile and ready laughter, her openness to unconventional ideas as well as to me—the unknown niece that she welcomed as if we'd known each other for ages—her airy clothing and ballet-style shoes. I'd never had a friend quite like her.

A friend. Is that what this new family member would become?

Only time would tell, I reminded myself. I pulled myself away from the window and set my cup aside, determined to make the most of the morning on my own. I showered, but decided the hair was going to be hopelessly bushy. It seemed to be doubling in volume in a purposeful effort to soak up as much moisture from this new climate as possible. I gave up attempts to style it and ended up pulling it back into a ponytail.

I thought of home. It would be good to check in with Ron at some point, make sure that things were under control at the office. Meaning that I hoped he wouldn't trash my office in an attempt to find a file or something that would, in fact, be buried on his own messy desk. I could also reassure him that Louisa seemed quite content without money from me. And then there was the longing to hear Drake's voice again. But a quick calculation of the time difference told me that this was not the hour to waken either of them.

Downstairs, the restaurant was bustling with people in business attire who seemed to be downing their final cups of coffee and heading out to important appointments. A willowy young server dressed all in black greeted me and I decided to treat myself to a full, traditional English breakfast. I won't sugar-coat this—I'm not one to stress over healthy eating. I tend to have what I want, and I'm lucky enough in the genetics department that I don't normally gain much weight. Either that or my tendency to run through life at a NASCAR pace keeps the pounds off. I gave this only about two seconds' thought as I cut into the first of the plump sausages on my plate.

A familiar shape approached, clad in waves of purple flowers.

"I thought I might catch you here," Louisa said. She slid into the chair opposite me but waved off the server's offer of food or drink. "I got a call early this morning. The woman who was to take the afternoon shift at the office is down with some kind of bug. I'm going to have to work all day."

"That's okay," I mumbled through the bite of toast that I'd just popped into my mouth. "I can find plenty of places to explore."

Her brows went into a little wrinkle. "I'm sure you'll be fine. I just feel like I'm abandoning you, and so quickly after your arrival."

I patted her hand. "It's fine. I've got my camera and there are a million pictures waiting to be taken out there."

"You're sure?"

"Positive. Don't worry about me."

"I'll be off work around four. Come by my place and I'll figure out something to make for dinner."

"I can take you out somewhere," I offered.

"Actually, I have some lovely fresh greens from my neighbor's garden. How about a salad? "

I gave a smile and a nod. After all, I supposed I shouldn't chow down on sausages and eggs *all* the time. Louisa rose, her quick little movements nearly upsetting a pitcher of milk, and she darted out the door after leaving me with the suggestion to come anytime and we could have tea in the garden. With a whiff of some exotic scent that matched the flowers on her dress, she was gone.

I leaned back in my chair and let the waitress take away my empty plate. I didn't see much of a change to my day; I'd planned to tour the Abbey and gardens, visit a few of the historic buildings, and take pictures up until lunch time anyway. With the large breakfast, I could foresee skipping lunch and maybe grabbing a nap before calling home sometime in the late afternoon. The kind of schedule a person on vacation *should* have.

By three o'clock I'd accomplished nearly everything on the list—including a tour inside the Gothic-style cathedral given by a very nice priest, minister, vicar, or whatever his title was. He never quite explained that. I'd managed enough photos to please the folks back home without, I hoped, boring them to death. The lure of the nap was beckoning as I unlocked the door to my room. I succumbed, only to be awakened by the phone's funny jangle an hour later.

"Hey babe," said Drake.

"What time is it there? I was going to call you later."

"It's way too early, for sure. But I have a flight so I was up at dawn. At the airport now, in fact. Just needed to hear your voice."

Aww. We exchanged mushy talk until I could hear the whine of rotor blades in the background. The routine of his flights had become so familiar to me that I could put myself right there in the cockpit with him, scanning the instruments and handling the controls. This past summer had included a little too much personal drama for me but I looked forward to working alongside him again. Soon, I hoped.

When the phone connection ended I realized that Louisa would be expecting me shortly. I straightened the mussed covers on the bed, swished some mouthwash to get rid of that sleep-taste, and ran a brush through my hair. Twenty minutes later I was again tapping the hefty brass knocker against the plate on her red front door.

She'd exchanged the flowered dress from this morning for a pair of stretchy leggings in lavender and a pretty top of filmy crepe-like fabric in what I was beginning to recognize as her signature colors of purple and aqua. This one had a pattern of tiny beads around the neckline.

I apologized for running a bit late, explaining about the phone call from Drake.

"It must be hard, juggling a man and a business," she said.

An image of myself trying to heft my husband into the air popped into my head. "Just juggling the man is tricky enough."

Her hearty laugh filled the room for a second. "Oh, you are so right about that!"

She ushered me through the parlor and into the kitchen.

"Tea and cake in the garden, or would you rather go straight to the wine and have an early dinner?" she asked. "I wasn't sure whether you've adjusted to the time change yet, so I'm prepared for either."

As tempting as the idea of a real English tea and cakes sounded, I had a feeling I needed something more substantial. After the big breakfast, and with all the midday activities, I had skipped lunch.

"Can I help you with the salad?" I asked, while she poured wine into two glasses.

"Everything's ready here on the worktop and it won't take but a moment."

"I would love to tour your garden," I said, peeping out the window in her back door.

"It's not terribly fancy, especially by English standards," she said. "Mostly roses."

We carried our wine glasses outside past a small bistro set, and I trailed her along a pathway of stepping stones as she showed off the last of the autumn blossoms, including a few hybrids that the home's previous owner had especially prized.

"Your mother loved roses, as I recall," she said, cupping a peachy bloom in one hand.

"She did. I've managed to keep quite a few of them alive but I'm not really a gardener." I'd already given her the quick rundown of how I'd inherited the house, during those get-acquainted conversations on the phone.

"I've kept a few of Arlene's letters. Last night after you left, I found them. Thought you might like to have them."

She moved on, pointing out some flowering border plants, but I found myself wrapping my mind around the idea of this whole other world of which I'd been completely unaware and the fact that my mother stayed in touch with Louisa even though my father would have surely disapproved.

We'd circled the tiny yard and arrived at the kitchen again before either of us spoke.

"A refill on your wine?" she asked, holding up the bottle and raising one eyebrow.

I'm rarely more than a one-glass person but I indicated the halfway mark on the glass.

"I'll just put the finishing touches on the salad, if you're ready."

I nodded. She rummaged in the fridge for something and I spotted a stack of envelopes beside the toaster. Plain white, but they were all rimmed with the red and blue stripes that used to be common on overseas mail.

"Are these—?" I tilted my head toward them.

"Oh! Yes, those are the ones I was telling you about. Take them."

I picked up the stack, probably a dozen of them at most. Across the fronts they were addressed in a familiar script that sent a pang through me. In the upper left corner of each was my address. The postal destinations changed. Nearest the top, there were a couple with Bury St. Edmunds addresses, but farther down I found ones that had been delivered in France, Switzerland, Italy and one in Morocco.

"You carried these with you all over the world, didn't you?"

She gave a far-off nostalgic smile.

As far as I knew, Mother hadn't kept any mementos from Louisa. Was it from fear of my father finding evidence of their friendship, or simply that she wasn't much of a packrat?

"Here we go, dear," Louisa said, carrying two heaping plates to the table. "In honor of your being here all the way from New Mexico, I've given this a little Southwestern flavor."

I hoped that I hid my misgivings about how well she might have accomplished that task. And it turned out that the salad was quite good, with fresh garden greens, black beans, corn, tomatoes, onion, a sprinkling of cheese over the top and a hint of chile-hot in the dressing. I savored the blend of flavors and when my initial hunger abated I finally posed the question that really had brought me here.

"Louisa, I have to ask . . . Why did I never know you existed?"

She toyed with the lettuce on her plate. "Bill and I were so different. Firstly, there was the age difference. He was already in college when I was born."

I remembered my father as tall, not quite stern but absolutely a no-nonsense man. He was most often preoccupied with his scientific work, an important job during the cold war years of the '60s. Even when he was with the family he wasn't really *with* us. His projects were more likely the place where his inner voice resided.

"Our parents were not ready to start over in raising another child. Funny, when I think back and do the math they were in their forties. Your grandmother was forty-two when I was born, your grandfather must have been forty-six. But he was one of those men who was old even when he was young." She cocked her head. "You know what I mean?"

I wagged my head vaguely. I didn't remember either of them.

"He walked like an old man, talked like one. He certainly had the attitudes of one. I was born to an era of rock 'n roll and poodle skirts and my father carried a pocket watch and wore a derby hat. In the western United States, where life tended toward the casual even then, he just seemed hopelessly stuffy."

She sipped from her wine and realized that the glass was empty, so she retrieved the bottle and topped her glass.

"Mother was never a well woman and she died while I was young. Father hired a nanny for me because he had no clue how to interact with a little girl. The nanny was even older than he, and I felt suffocated in that house. In my teens I have to confess I went a little wild. Started drinking, tried a little marijuana, played the music as loud as I could.

"Anyhow, Bill, your dad, always seemed a lot like your grandpa to me. Bill had married and moved his family to Albuquerque so he could take that government job. Your brothers were young and your mom was expecting you, and then I dropped the bombshell on the family that I was pregnant. Father hit the roof. Bill read me the riot act. Together they planned my life for me. I would enter a home for unwed girls and give the baby up for adoption. I could finish my last semester of high school courses in that place then enter college on schedule with the rest of my friends. No one would know of the family shame because the cover story was that I was going to live with my married brother's family and attend college there."

"Did you? Actually live with us?"

Our plates were empty and we pushed them to the middle of the table.

"Their plan worked up to a point. I had no choice about the girl's home. Father drove me there and hauled me inside. The place actually had grills over the windows and a ten-foot brick wall around the grounds. It wasn't quite prison but it might as well have been. Unlucky me, I was having morning sickness so badly that I couldn't even think about jumping the wall until it was way too late. So I resigned myself to stay there those seven awful months. But I also resolved that I would never, ever, ever go back to either my father's house or my brother's."

"What about the baby's father?"

"Never really in the picture. By the time I was certain of the pregnancy he had dropped me for another girl. We weren't meant to be together."

She swallowed hard and her eyes welled up. "They never even let me see the baby. A nice married couple had already signed papers agreeing to take him the day he was born. I heard that there was a nursery on premises where doctors looked after the newborns until they were released to go home, but I never saw the place. For all I know they took him the minute they'd bathed him and put his first diaper on."

She let out a long pent-up breath. "Silly, now, after all this time. That little boy is pretty close to your age, and I have no idea where he has ended up. Nothing to be done about it from my standpoint. I'm sure he had a happy life, and it's certain that it was a more stable life than I could have ever given him. So, no regrets."

She stood and carried the plates to the sink.

"But neither your father nor mine ever forgave you for what now seems like a very minor 'sin'?"

"In the beginning it was that way. Both of them wanted to lecture me, to control me. It was I who couldn't forgive them." She picked up her wine glass and tilted her head toward the parlor. I followed her and settled into one end of the sofa.

"Seriously, now with hindsight, I know that giving up

the baby was the right thing. It was the principle, that I was forced into the decision with no input. They absolutely did not care how I felt about it."

"What did you do?"

"I took off. I'd hoarded the spending money my father had put on account for me at the home. Used it for a bus ticket to New York. Waited tables until I could afford a standby ticket to Paris. Gosh, I was so lucky. It never occurred to me that I could end up homeless or working some street corner. I landed in Paris and went into a restaurant to apply for a job. No idea that a foreigner needs certain documents to get a job. The couple who owned this place were ex-pat Americans and they took me in. Let me work and live above the café. I saved my money, traveled all I wanted to, always had their place to go home to. More wine?"

I declined. My head felt woozy already. "Louisa! You really did get lucky."

She laughed that hearty laugh of hers. "I really did. There were some sad times. It wasn't long before I heard about Father's death. I never made peace with him. And then when I heard about Bill and Arlene—that's when it really hit me that I should have probably settled things with both of them."

"But it was done by then."

She nodded. "It was. I wrote to your brother and expressed regrets."

"And I'm so sorry that he never responded. None of us were angry with you, believe me. We simply never knew."

"I know, dear. I know." She moved to my end of the sofa and gave me a hug, then picked up the wine glasses and headed toward the kitchen. "I'm only glad that we've now made connection."

I listened to the clinking of glassware in the kitchen and made my decision. Standing in the doorway and watching her set things into the sink, I spoke. "Louisa, I really would like to stay here after all."

Chapter 5

She set me up in the guest room with the loan of a nightshirt and a new toothbrush. We both decided it was hardly worth the effort to walk back to the hotel tonight. It was getting late and a heavy fog blanketed the streets, making the pavement and stone surfaces look glossy and slick.

"Perfect atmosphere for my 'haunted Bury' tour," Louisa said, peering out the window as she lowered the shade. "Too bad I don't have another one scheduled until next Saturday."

She turned to me. "No rush to get up in the morning. Catch up on your sleep. I have to put in a couple of hours at the tourism office, just until noon, then we'll have the whole afternoon to play." She sent an air kiss my direction and bade me goodnight as she closed my door. I eased beneath the soft comforter and must have fallen asleep in something like four seconds.

The smell of coffee wafted through the air and I rolled over to peek at my watch, which I'd left on the nightstand. It was after seven. With a quick change back into last night's clothes, a splash of cool water on my face, and a borrowed half-inch of my aunt's toothpaste I felt ready to start a new day.

Louisa sat at the kitchen table in her robe, holding a newspaper, with a steaming mug in front of her.

"Help yourself to coffee, dear, or the kettle's always ready for tea, if you'd prefer that. I love my tea later in the day but can't seem to start my engine without coffee first," she said. "Sleep well?"

"Like a dead woman. I don't think I rolled over even once." I reached for the carafe, one of the few post-1950s touches in the house. She'd left a clean mug on the worktop for me, alongside a small silver bowl filled with sugar cubes and silver tongs to grab them with and a matching pitcher containing—I guessed—real cream. I indulged in all of it.

"I don't generally keep everything for a full English breakfast here," she said, folding the newspaper to the back page. "But we could certainly go out for that if you'd like. Otherwise, there are some store-bought muffins or toast—buttered or with cinnamon." Her eyes sparkled. "I make a killer cinnamon toast."

"That would be perfect."

I watched as she sliced bread, slathered it with butter and gave it a generous sprinkling of sugar and cinnamon before placing it on a baking sheet under the gas flame broiler. The resulting combination of soft bread and crunchy topping literally melted in my mouth.

"Have you thought of selling this stuff and making yourself a fortune?" I mumbled while trying to lick sugar crystals off my lips.

She laughed. "Too much paperwork to start a business. Besides, this way I keep my house guests coming back."

She asked about my life back in Albuquerque although we'd covered some of this ground over the phone before my visit, the parts about my involvement in both Ron's private investigation firm and Drake's helicopter service.

"And he's actually taught you how to pilot one?" she asked.

I nodded and watched a proud twinkle come into her eyes.

"The last few months I have to admit that I've only flown enough to stay current. There hasn't been enough business to keep both of us flying right now. The economy. It's the reason he had to stay home now." Thinking of Drake made me realize that if he'd tried to call my hotel room last night I wasn't there and he might be concerned about that. I wished that I'd made arrangements for cell service over here.

"You are certainly welcome to use my telephone," Louisa said when I mentioned it.

"Later. It must be the middle of the night back there right now."

She bustled about, tidying the kitchen, saying that she'd better dress. Fifteen minutes later, ready to leave for the office, she told me to feel free to use her car to bring my belongings from the hotel. The mere idea of negotiating the narrow lanes, many of which were one-way and finding my way back again without damage to the car set my stomach on edge. She handed me a spare house key and I assured her that I could wheel my bag behind me and make it back here.

By eleven, I'd accomplished all that, checking out of the hotel without a problem although I had a little twinge as I said goodbye to my room in the famed old building. I spread out and made my few possessions at home in Louisa's guest room, then decided to drop back in at The Knit and Purl and buy the cloth purse I'd seen there for Elsa. There was still plenty of time before meeting Louisa at noon at the tourism office.

Undoubtedly there was a more direct route, but as I still didn't have a clear map of the town in my head I found myself using the Angel Hotel as my reference point. I walked the increasingly familiar route back to it, then remembered the way Louisa and I had taken the previous afternoon to the knit shop.

Once again the small bells tinkled as I opened the door. No one was visible in the shop but I could hear voices from a back room.

"Hello?" I called out.

"Be there in a moment." Dolly peered around a corner from the other room. She gave me that look that says I think I know you but am not quite sure.

"Charlie Parker," I reminded. "I was in with my aunt Louisa."

"Oh, yes." Her mouth was pinched in a tight grimace. "Give us a moment. Louisa's yarn came in this morning. Gabrielle can get it for you. We've had a little mishap."

I followed her glance downward and saw that she was holding an ice pack against her right hand. Another female voice spoke to her and Dolly turned to give the girl some instructions.

A young woman came out—early twenties, slightly plump, with a peachy complexion and honey blond hair held up with a clip. She held about ten skeins of heather blue yarn, which she set on the counter near the register.

Dolly introduced her as Gabrielle Tukson, her assistant.

"Afraid we've had an accident," Gabrielle said. "Dolly's gotten a rather nasty burn, just a few minutes ago."

Dolly had trailed behind the employee, watching how she handled the expensive yarn and pointing at a price sheet with her injured hand. A brilliant red blotch showed near the intersection of thumb and index finger and spread across the back of her hand.

"Ow, that does look painful. What happened?" I asked.

Dolly replaced the ice pack over the red spot. "Tea. I'd just set down a cup that had gone cold, turned to switch on the kettle and make a fresh cup, went back to pick up the cold cup and it was scalding hot. Dropped it, I did. The rim burnt my fingertips and the rest sloshed over my hand."

"How on earth—?"

Dolly stared at the injured hand, her mouth now in a hard line. "It's just one more unexplained thing around this shop, I tell you."

Could Louisa be right about a poltergeist?

Gabrielle had placed the blue yarn into a bag. "The other thing that's upset her so is that the cup broke when she dropped it and it was a favorite," she said quietly.

"It most certainly was! One from my own grandmother's set of Spode—her Billingsly Rose pattern. I'm sick about it. Just sick."

"That's too bad," I said. "Do you need to see a doctor for your hand?"

Gabrielle gave me a look that said she'd already suggested that.

"I'll be all right," Dolly insisted.

Still visibly upset, she elbowed her assistant aside and asked whether I wanted to take Louisa's yarn with me now.

"I actually came in to buy a purse that I saw before," I said. "Maybe it would be better if Louisa and I came back later, let you take care of that burn first. I'm sure there's not a hurry on the yarn and I can get the purse anytime."

"Oh, nonsense," Dolly said with a big smile. Clearly she didn't want to see a sure sale walk out the door. "Gabrielle can help you with your purchase, and Louisa can come by anytime to pay for her yarn. I'm not concerned about it."

She reached for a small receipt book and winced as her hand brushed against the edge of the cash register.

I reached for my wallet. "It's the yellow one with the brown trim and short handles," I told Gabrielle.

She wrapped it in tissue and placed a foil sticker with the shop's emblem to hold the edges of the paper together. Dolly watched the process but she was clearly in pain and when I mentioned again that she might want to see the doctor she didn't protest.

Outside, the day had turned warm. Sunshine hit the narrow lane and illuminated the wares in the shops. I strolled slowly along, absorbing the same-yet-different feel of a foreign town—books with sticker prices in pounds, clothing somehow more stylish than ours, newspaper headlines eerily similar to those in the States that featured corrupt politicians, brutal crimes, and the latest foibles of movie stars. By the time I'd meandered my way back to Abbeygate

Street, the one place I was beginning to recognize, it was nearing twelve so I angled toward the tourism office where Louisa worked.

She sat behind a counter in the gift shop. I said hello and handed over the bag from The Knit and Purl with her blue yarn in it.

"Charlie! So glad you found me. Let me introduce you to my co-worker, Alice."

An older woman stepped forward, smiling and nodding, and I got the feeling she knew more about me than I could possibly guess. Either that or she just had a slight tremor and her head nodded all the time anyway. She greeted me so politely that I felt obliged to let her show me around the shop as she pointed out the various maps and brochures a person could take for free.

"Your aunt conducts the best tours of anyone," she told me in her high, proper voice. "The historical talks are marvelous but I especially like the scary ones!"

I had to chuckle at the way her eyes lit up at the mention of the haunted sites.

Louisa had put on her jacket and she placed a hand on Alice's shoulder. "We need to be going now. Can you handle things until Hazel gets here?"

Alice nodded some more.

"What do you feel like having for lunch?" Louisa asked once we'd stepped out into the sunshine again.

While it was tempting to go for a repeat at the Cornish pasty shop and another walk in the gardens, I realized that my time was limited here and it would be fun to try some different places. I told her I would defer to her recommendation. And so we found ourselves at The Dog and Partridge, a pub dating back to the 16th century.

"This place is on my tour," Louisa said as we took seats at a table in the corner after placing our orders for fish and chips at the bar. "However, I won't bore you with the details now."

I shrugged my jacket over the back of my chair. "Speaking of the unexplained . . ." I went on to tell her about Dolly's unfortunate mishap with the cup of scalding tea. "She swears she'd just set the cup down and that the tea was stone cold."

Louisa listened raptly. "It's at least the third time, assuming she's told me about all these events, since they moved into that shop. With the frequency . . . well, it's as if some spirit doesn't want her in that location. It's quite common, you know, for spirits to appear to new tenants. They don't always like us in their space."

I could think of possible explanations for each event. Perhaps Dolly had become so wrapped up in her work that she'd forgotten she'd already reheated her tea. The inventory of yarn being completely rearranged during the night was a little more complicated. Dolly obviously didn't accidentally do it, which would suggest that someone had quietly sneaked into her shop. Certainly not impossible, but how likely? More likely than there being ghosts in the building. Just my opinion.

Our fish and chips arrived and I put all other thoughts out of my mind as I ripped into the huge piece of battered fish that was done to perfection. The fries—I couldn't quite think of them as chips yet—were hot and crispy, and we didn't speak much for about ten minutes.

Louisa reached a stopping place first, wiped her fingers on her napkin and peeked into the yarn sack I'd given her earlier.

"Do you mind if we stop by Dolly's again so I can pay her for this?" she asked.

I let out a sigh of contentment. The traditional lunch had hit just the right spot for me. "You know, I was wondering . . . do you think the pranks at the shop might have anything to do with the fact that Halloween is coming up?"

She sipped from the Coke she'd ordered and thought about it. "It's still more than a month away. Someone would really be getting an early start."

"Do people here do all the same things we used to do?"

"Pretty much. Mostly harmless and fun things— costumes, parties and treats, lots of orange and black, carved pumpkins, scary movies. The wearing of costumes goes back to pagan times when people believed that troubled spirits moved about at this time of year. They disguised themselves to avoid being recognized by the undead."

I smiled at the memory of the year I'd dressed up as a witch when I was about eight, thought I was the meanest thing on the streets until some bigger kid in a space alien costume practically scared the pants off me and chased me home.

"So, you probably give a heck of a haunted sites tour that night," I teased.

"You bet! I take along a couple of assistants who can escort the terminally frightened back to their cars."

"Well, even though I won't be here next month, I'd love to see the places while I'm here."

"I'll put you on the list for my Saturday night tour. Meanwhile, there are some good spots on our way back to Dolly's." She slipped her jacket back on and picked up her shopping bag.

We stepped out to the street again and Louisa led the way diagonally across the intersection toward St. Mary's Church.

"St. Mary's was completed in 1427 and is the burial place of Mary Tudor, daughter of King Henry the Eighth. This area is famous for sightings of two ghosts, the Grey Lady and the Brown Monk. I'll cover more about them on my tour."

Beside the brown stone church a pathway led into a graveyard where long grass grew over and among the graves. Tilted headstones dotted the uneven ground, not a place where you could safely assume you weren't walking over *someone's* grave. A small stone building sat in the midst of them, surrounded by a high iron fence painted black. I wandered over to take a look at the many plaques attached to it.

"This is the Charnel House," Louisa said, "built in the 13th century to store the bones of some of the graveyard's inhabitants."

I read some fascinating inscriptions, including one about a nine-year-old girl killed by a flash of lightning as she prayed. So, church might not necessarily be the safest place to hang out, I decided.

Louisa told more stories and pointed out that some of the graves had both head and foot markers at either end of their stone sarcophagi. "I can go on with minutiae for two whole hours, but you'd probably rather cover a little more ground than this single square block."

I skirted the lumps in the ground that felt like they undoubtedly contained bones and we made our way back to the paved path. A lone young woman was walking toward us in the shade of the huge trees. Surrounded by the church, the abbey and high walls, with the path that disappeared around a curve in the distance, I could easily imagine making that same journey on a dark, foggy night. A scatter of goose-bumps rose along my arms.

Chapter 6

The sunshine had dimmed behind thick clouds and I pulled my blazer a little tighter around me as Louisa led the way back toward the street. Cars zipped by on the narrow street and the shouts of school children came from somewhere nearby. The moody feel of the graveyard dissipated in a flash.

Louisa glanced up at the sky. "Got your brolly?"

I patted my oversized purse. The umbrella never got any use in New Mexico but I had a feeling it would come in handy here.

However, by the time we reached The Knit and Purl's front door the wind had shifted and the clouds were thinning again. Warm light glowed from the shop windows and I could see Gabrielle inside, flicking at the rows of candles on the shelves with a feather duster. She smiled at us when we walked in.

"Dolly's up in the apartment," she said. "Go on up if you'd like."

Louisa knew the way and I followed along, through a good-sized stockroom lined with shelves and up a flight of uneven stairs, a reminder of the age of even the most simple buildings in this town. Ahead of me, she'd come to a landing and before she could knock at the door a shriek pierced the silence.

Louisa gazed around with momentary confusion. With no qualms, I barreled ahead of her, grabbed the doorknob and shoved my way into the apartment. I found myself alone in a parlor similar in size to the one at Louisa's house.

"Dolly!" I shouted. "Where are you?"

She bustled in from a doorway to my right, her hands fluttering, confusion on her face.

"It's another one!" she cried.

I stared around the room and through the open door to the kitchen. "Another what?"

Louisa had followed me inside and she rushed to her friend. "What is it, pet?"

Dolly's voice didn't want to work.

"Take a deep breath," I said.

Archie, the husband I'd briefly met yesterday, appeared from a hallway on the left. His hair was mussed, as if he'd just woken from a nap. "Dolly, what is it, love?"

Dolly's eyes scanned our faces, her mouth working without saying anything.

"Breathe," I reminded.

She finally focused on me and I breathed deeply, hoping she would imitate me. She did and finally calmed down enough to speak.

"The tea. Again. Just like yesterday."

I automatically glanced down at her hands but didn't see a new injury.

"This time it went cold. My tea went ice cold in less than two minutes."

We all stared at her.

"It's true. I'd just made a fresh cup. I'll show you!" She led the little procession into the kitchen. "See? The kettle is still hot. I had poured a cup." She pointed to a solid white mug on the counter. "I felt the, well, the call of nature . . . went to the loo. I was not gone two minutes. When I came back—well, just feel this."

Call me suspicious but I held my hand above the cup for a second before actually touching it. When I did, I had to agree with Dolly, the liquid was actually ice cold.

I looked around the room, not exactly sure what I was hoping to see. "And there was no one in the apartment but you and Archie?"

"He'd laid down for his nap after lunch," she said, glancing toward him for confirmation. He nodded.

The electric kettle, indeed, still emitted a tendril of steam when I poured some of the water into the sink. The tea in the mug had not come from this source, not recently. Puzzling.

"I felt a rush of cold air come through the parlor as I left the toilet," she was telling Louisa. "But this place can be drafty. I didn't think anything of it."

Louisa nodded knowingly. "The spirits are often associated with cold drafts."

Archie clearly would rather get back to his nap. He seemed torn between comforting his wife and getting out of the roomful of women. Eventually he just patted her shoulder and edged his way out of the room.

Louisa speculated about the rash of unexplained incidents, while Dolly insisted she'd only been startled, that she hadn't sustained another injury. I walked around the kitchen looking for real clues as to what might have happened. I have to admit, nothing seemed out of place.

Dolly had regained her composure and now she squared her thin shoulders. "Well. This is becoming ridiculous. I have a shop to run. I'd best get back to it."

We trooped down the stairs single file and I wandered over to the display of herbs and essential oils while Louisa completed the mission that had brought us here, paying for her yarn order. Gabrielle had finished dusting the candles and was now rearranging the display.

"Everything all right up there?" she asked, obviously not so worried about her employer that she felt the necessity of interrupting her work.

I gave a quick explanation of what had happened.

"Did Mr. Jones see it too, then?"

"Only after the fact, like we did. Mainly, we just interrupted his nap."

She nodded, a soft smile on her face.

"Ready to move onward, Charlie?" Louisa stood near the door, and it appeared that Dolly was once more in full control behind the register.

I said quick goodbyes to the two women and joined Louisa on the sidewalk.

"I want to pop over to Marks and Spencer for a couple of grocery items," she said. "Thought maybe we'd just do a light dinner at home tonight."

That sounded appealing. My jeans weren't going to take kindly to a lot more of those fish-and-chips meals.

"What's the story with Archie Jones?" I asked as we

walked along. "He seems young to be retired, home napping in the middle of the day."

"Ah. It's a little bit of a sore point with Dolly. He used to be a manager at the sugar factory. Got laid off more than a year ago and hasn't found anything else. They lived on the outskirts of town, nice modern house. Had to rent it out and move to the empty apartment above the shop."

"That probably didn't set too well with him, either."

"Not at all well. First, he wanted Dolly to sell the shop. Fumed over how much she'd spent to set it up in the first place. But she did that with her own money, something she came into when her father died. Dolly just put her foot down, said she was at least bringing in some money and if Archie couldn't go out and get himself another job then he'd best start helping out around the shop."

I could imagine *that* conversation hitting the fan.

"So, I suppose that's what he does now. Unpacks cartons of inventory, washes the windows, that sort of thing."

I pictured the soft-spoken man with his slumped shoulders. I could more easily see him washing windows than in a management role with a big company.

As if she'd read my mind, Louisa continued. "You'd hardly have recognized Archie two years ago. Top of the world, suit and tie every day, business lunches at the best restaurants and trips all over the country. Kind of sad, really, how his self esteem was so closely tied to that job. The longer he's away from it the more stooped he becomes. Lucky for them, really, that they had Dolly's shop."

She pointed at an entry on our right. "Here we are."

I followed her around the food market section of the store, eyeing the bakery items that would be new to my palate, thinking this would be a good place to stop by on my own, pick up a few things to take home. She chose fresh lettuce and tomatoes, along with some veggies.

"I should have thought of this Saturday," she remarked. "Market day on the square, and things would have been bargain priced. Plus, you would have had a taste of a tradition that's been going here for a thousand years."

I expressed regret but she assured me we could catch it on Wednesday. Her purchases filled a plastic shopping bag, which I offered to carry since she still had the yarn.

"I'd intended to show you one more local landmark, The Nutshell Pub, which is known as the smallest pub in Britain, but perhaps we should take these things home first. You might be up for a little rest, yourself?"

The rain that managed to hold off more than half the day hit with a vengeance as soon as we walked into the house so our plan for the little pub got postponed. The downpour settled into a steady drizzle while Louisa napped. Restless, I wasn't sleepy and found myself pacing through the parlor, once again taking stock of the books on the shelves.

I suspected that the collection had, for the most part, belonged to the previous owner just like the rest of the furnishings. There were classic novels of the Bronte sisters' era and several volumes on gardening, a pastime Louisa had admitted to me that she did not much indulge in. One of her neighbors loved the hobby so much that he came over to keep her roses fed and pruned and the scrap of lawn trimmed, and she was perfectly happy with that.

The one section that no doubt came to the house with my aunt was a corner shelf filled with books on astrology, the occult, and histories of ghostly doings in and around

the town of Bury. I pulled one down and flipped through
the pages. It was an excellent reference and I could see
why Louisa was now considered such an authority on her
tours—she'd really done her research.

A small booklet slipped from between two of the
guidebooks and fell to the floor. Wrinkled from humidity
and yellowed with age, it clearly was of a different vintage
from the other books nearby. When I bent to pick it up, I
saw that it was titled in a foreign language—something that
looked a bit like German but with a whole lot of diacritical
markings. Hmm . . . A crude hand drawing of a hooded
figure decorated the front cover. I flipped through the pages
and a single sheet of folded paper popped out. More of the
foreign writing. The rain blasted the windows with renewed
vigor, casting the room in a wavering light.

"Charlie?"

I jumped about a mile and I think a squeak escaped me.
"Louisa! I'm so sorry. I didn't mean to snoop—"

She gave me a quizzical look. "I was about to ask if
you'd like some tea. Did you get to nap at all?"

I shook my head and closed the booklet. "I was looking
at some of your books about the haunted sites here in Bury
and I—this—well, it fell off the shelf."

Don't get me wrong. I am an incurable snooper. It's just
that I itch a little when I actually get caught at it.

Louisa patted my arm on her way to the kitchen.
"Charlie, it's fine. Help yourself to anything you see. I tend
to keep an eclectic mix."

I heard her fill the kettle and take mugs from the
cupboard.

"So, then can I ask—what's this language?" I stood in
the doorway and held up the booklet.

"Oh, that. It's Romanian." She spooned loose tea into a ceramic pot. A dreamy look came over her face. "Nicolae gave me the book. Right before I had to escape. That single sheet was the forged document that was supposed to keep me from the firing squad. I could have fallen in love with that man—dark curly hair, vivid blue eyes . . ." She sighed. "I really missed him."

"Romanian. Wait—escape? Seriously?"

The kettle whistled and she poured boiling water over the tea leaves and set the lid in place on the teapot.

"Of course, dear. Well, in those days one didn't simply ask the communists to let you go. But there was a pretty well established underground movement, a few days dodging through the woods. It wasn't really cold that time of year. Except on rainy nights. And of course I always questioned whether that document would have really saved me."

While she spilled out this matter-of-fact recount, she brought out a plate and opened a package of cookies that she'd bought earlier.

"So you escaped from communist Romania in the dark of night . . . What were you doing there in the first place?"

"Oh. Well that, of course, was because I'd gone to Transylvania. My interest in eastern European witchcraft." She caught my incredulous stare. "I gave it up after a couple of years. Fascinating people, but it was sort of a crowded field."

I think my expression conveyed the *What??* that was going through my mind. She smiled sweetly and I couldn't help it. I burst into giggles. Once I started, she practically collapsed with laughter herself.

"Oh, I can *so* understand why my father could not accept your lifestyle."

"I know—" she gasped. "Silly, isn't it? Bill and me, brother and sister. It really never quite worked."

I sank into one of the chairs at the kitchen table. Once I caught my breath, I had to ask. "So, what's the book about? Can you actually read it?"

"I used to. I'm probably fairly rusty at it now." She poured tea into the two mugs and set them on the table. "It's a book of spells."

Ah. I reached for a cookie to keep myself from cracking up again.

"If you noticed the little wooden box on the shelf . . . the compartments in it contain the basics that a witch needs—eye of newt and such."

"And did you have a wand?" I asked.

Her brows drew together in the middle. "Well, no, of course not."

Chapter 7

I pulled myself from my snug little nest of blankets and was shocked to find that I'd slept close to twelve hours despite the fact that I'd gone to bed with images of Louisa sneaking through a forest in Eastern Europe under threat of death. I found clean jeans and a pullover top and decided a ponytail was the easy answer for my hair. A couple of swipes with the blusher and lipstick and I felt as ready as I'd ever be.

In the kitchen, Louisa sat at the table with her coffee, newspaper and toast.

"You look chipper," she said. "I guess you slept all right?"

"That bed is wonderful. I may have to steal it and take it home with me." I helped myself to coffee from the carafe.

"I'm off to work in a bit, but make yourself at home.

It looks like Bethany will be out again. Unless I can find a replacement I probably can't break away before four o'clock."

"Not a problem. I thought I'd explore a little bit more, pick up some gifts to take home."

There were two bookshops we'd passed in our strolls yesterday and I thought I could probably find something for my brother's three young sons there. Better to encourage reading, I felt, than video games. For Drake, one of the clothing stores' display windows held a selection of men's wear and I might investigate that a bit further.

Louisa bustled around the kitchen, putting an apple and a sandwich into a bag to take with her, offering me the run of the kitchen if I wanted to eat lunch in.

"Choose a nice place for dinner tonight," I told her. "My treat." With what I was now saving on hotel costs I should be treating her to gourmet meals every night.

She hurried out the door, while I lingered over my coffee. I wondered how I would adapt to life in such a home—fitted tightly between neighboring places, a tiny garden outside the back door, the front leading directly to the road—but the small rooms and low ceilings made it amazingly cozy and warm against the damp climate. Last night Louisa had lit the gas fireplace in the parlor while we watched TV and the little room had warmed quickly.

I took one more glance at the items on her bookshelf, including a peek into the potion box. Fascinating stuff, but I had other things in mind for the day. I stuck the box back in its spot and gathered my purse, umbrella and the little guide map Louisa's co-worker had insisted I take along yesterday.

Waterstone's Books was easy to find and I lost myself in the stacks, picking up the British edition of a favorite

American author's newest book to read in my spare moments during the vacation, then moving on to the children's section where I spent way too much time stressing over what each of Ron's boys would enjoy. Eventually I took the recommendation of a young clerk who told me which titles were the hottest things locally for kids. Maybe the boys would be impressed enough to give them a try.

On to the clothing store where I found a casual jacket I thought Drake would love. Warm enough for our high-desert seasons and dressy enough that he might actually take to wearing it when we went out in the evenings.

At the checkout desk, I spotted a familiar posture. Archie Jones.

"Is Dolly's hand feeling better?" I asked.

He visibly started, shoving a packet of something that looked like underwear behind his back. His brow wrinkled as he concentrated on figuring out where he'd seen me.

"Charlie Parker, Louisa's niece."

"Oh yes, quite. Dolly is doing much better, thank you. I insisted she keep the ice on it for a few hours immediately after, you know. The redness is completely gone now, I'm happy to say."

The clerk was waiting for one of us to take the lead so he could ring up a purchase. Archie gestured for me to go first. I placed the jacket on the counter and turned back to him. "And her scare? Upstairs in the kitchen?"

"She's not mentioned it again. Dolly's such a trouper, you know. Brushes off those types of things and moves on with her day."

"Well, I'm glad to hear it."

I paid for the jacket with a credit card and moved toward the street exit but before I got to the door a table piled with sweaters caught my eye. I paused to imagine a certain forest-green one on Drake and noticed that Archie was conversing quietly with the clerk but his glance edged toward me frequently. Maybe he didn't really want to get roped into further conversation with me. I set the sweater aside and left.

I considered window shopping on the way back to Louisa's house but my packages were becoming heavy so I headed directly there, dropped them off, then went back out. The day had turned nice again, with warm sun and only a light breeze. I took a deep breath and savored the charm of the narrow lane stretching beyond me in both directions. A little pang—it would have been more fun to explore this with Drake. But I was here and he wasn't, so I might as well make the best of it. At least I was getting plenty of exercise.

I took off in the direction opposite my accustomed route to the shops and found myself deeper in a small residential neighborhood, on a street that curved steadily to my right. Just before I began to wonder whether I was becoming hopelessly lost a familiar-looking intersection appeared and I realized it was Lilac Lane, where I'd walked a dozen times already and that The Knit and Purl was almost directly across the street from me.

Dolly was at the front glass, working on a window display. She spotted me and waved. I crossed the narrow road and walked over and she beckoned me to come inside.

"How are you today?" I asked as the door closed behind me.

She pursed her lips, about to say something, but changed her mind.

"I'm fine, thanks." She held up the hand that had been

scalded to show me that none of the redness remained. She pushed up the sleeves of her sweater and glanced around the empty shop. "Be better, though, if I had more customers. Do you suppose they're hearing about these incidents and that's keeping them away?"

"Oh, I wouldn't think so. If anything, having a haunted shop would bring more customers in, wouldn't it? Well, it would in the States. Hotels and restaurants there seem to capitalize on their ghosts."

She raised one angular shoulder. "I dunno. Only seems it's been slow lately. I let Gabrielle have the day off to go see her sister in Stowmarket. No point in two of us being here. Do you think this display is appealing? Thought the bright colored yarns would draw the eye."

"It certainly caught my eye," I said, in a small attempt to cheer her up. "It's very nice."

She didn't look completely convinced. "If I could just find out what's really going on around here. We only moved into this spot about a year ago. I've heard of cases where an old ghost doesn't like a new tenant and tries to scare the occupant away. Makes me wonder."

"You could ask Louisa. She's knowledgeable about which buildings in town are reputed to be haunted." Personally, I thought it a lot more likely that a human would have an agenda than a ghost. "Maybe the previous tenant left something behind and is trying to come back for it."

"Like what? Wouldn't they walk right in the door and just ask me for it?" She picked up some skeins that she hadn't used in the window display and carried them to the wall of shelving that held her inventory. "The place was rather cluttered when we took over, especially the cellar. Loads of old empty boxes, some construction materials. We never found anything of value when we cleared it all away."

What *would* someone leave behind that they couldn't come back and request? My mind immediately went to thoughts of a hidden stash of something—valuables, drugs, contraband?

"What kind of shop was it before you moved in?"

"Charity thrift store," she said. "You've noticed them around town, I'm sure. The Heart Association, the Cancer Fund and such. I think this one was something to do with Alzheimer's Research."

I couldn't help it. I chuckled. "So there you have it. They've forgotten what it was they left behind."

Finally, a smile from her. But it faded quickly. Obviously she still believed that anyone coming for their possessions would simply walk in the door and ask. And she could be right.

"When Archie gets home from his business meeting I'll ask him to check around in the cellar some more. Perhaps we can figure this out."

"A meeting?" I blurted it out without thinking, realizing the mistake when her face turned to ice. "I'm sorry. It's not my business." Archie hadn't been dressed in business attire when I saw him buying new underwear awhile ago.

"It's all right." Her tone stayed a little frosty. "The meeting was really an interview. That's all."

"But—" I stopped. She obviously didn't know where her husband was. "I understand. And really—I won't say a word."

"It's not like it's anything to be ashamed of," she said, pulling her shoulders straighter. "In these times . . . Besides, he's been an enormous help in getting my shop set up and all. Really, we're a team now. I prefer it this way."

"Good. That's great." I felt my face freeze into a falsely bright smile.

She covered by stepping behind the register and tamping some papers into a neat stack; I covered by picking up a random candle and telling her I'd meant to buy it yesterday. I paid for the candle and put it into my purse.

"Charlie," she said as I turned to leave. "Louisa told me that you are a private detective, in your home city."

Oh, god, here it comes, I thought. That inevitable request. That faint hope that I might find the answers to someone's problems. I recognized the look on her face. What could I say? It would be supremely ungracious of me to turn down the request, having already pulled one social gaffe within the past five minutes.

"Do you think you could discover what is happening here? In my shop. Why these pranks. Low-key, of course. I don't want any more patrons frightened away."

"I'll see what I can do." And with that, I sealed my fate.

Chapter 8

I set my purse down and perched on a stool near the counter. I could at least ask some questions.

"You haven't reported any of these incidents to the authorities?" I asked, knowing the answer already.

"I thought about reporting a break-in when I found that someone had moved all the wools," she said, "but I imagined the constable's reaction. Nothing was missing."

True. What crime had really occurred? Malicious rearrangement?

"The two incidents with the teacups . . . well, had someone told me the story I would have said they got busy and forgot what they'd done, had let time slip away."

I nodded slowly, trying to find a logical answer to this. "Okay, let's assume someone has come into the shop and is using these pranks to cover other activities. Has any other merchandise or money been missing? Have there been any other occasions when something was out of place?"

Dolly shook her head more vigorously with each question I posed.

I walked over to the shop's door and examined it. Not that I'm any kind of expert, but I couldn't see any marks on either the lock or the wood, nothing to indicate it had been tampered with.

"Is there another entrance to the apartment upstairs or does a person have to come through the shop?"

She led me to the street and pointed out a narrow door I'd not previously noticed. The wooden door was painted a glossy black and there was a mail slot in it. Above the door were three small window panes. "There are stairs to the upper floor here. But this door is locked all the time. Archie and I use the inside stairs exclusively."

"Do you receive your mail through this slot?"

"No. Normally the postman carries our personal post in with that for the shop. He knows who we are so he hands me the entire stack—business and personal."

I twisted at the knob on the black door. As Dolly had told me, it was securely locked.

"May I see the cellar?"

We went back into the shop and she took me through the stockroom and opened another door. A flight of stone steps led downward. She flipped a switch on the wall, illuminating them.

"I'd better stay with the shop, but take your time. There's another switch at the bottom which lights up the entire cellar. It's one large room." She stepped aside to let me pass. "And, Charlie? Thank you."

I reached the bottom of the steps and stared into the

cluttered space, unsure where to begin. Most of the single, large room was filled with furniture. Presumably, belonging to Archie and Dolly. Otherwise she would have mentioned that the previous tenant left it. Louisa had told me that they owned a large house on the outskirts of town but it was now occupied by renters. They must have needed a place for their excess furniture and this was it. Boxes were stacked upon dressers; bedding in plastic zip bags sat on a pair of overstuffed leather chairs. The matching sofa was empty except for a couple of neatly folded afghans, which might have been overstock from the shop. One entire wall was hidden by stacks of packing boxes, labeled with household descriptions like "Library - books," "Kitchen – spare pots and pans" and "Dining Room." Dolly had probably chosen the items she most needed every day, limiting herself to what the small upstairs apartment could accommodate, and packed away the remaining things.

The fact that she hadn't merely sold the excess at the time of the move told me that they must have had plans to eventually move back to the larger digs. No wonder Archie felt the pressure to get back to work.

To the left of the wall of boxes I spotted something out of place. A section of the stone floor had been lifted and the dirt beneath it looked freshly disturbed, a bit damp. Someone had obviously been digging there but I saw no tools nearby. I stooped to examine the spot but there wasn't a single gold coin or bag of jewels to be found. I brushed the dirt from my hands. So much for the hope of easy treasure.

A little farther along the wall an area about five feet high and four feet wide was made of brick. All the other walls were limestone or rock. I touched the bricks tentatively, half expecting a secret doorway to swing open and a mummy or something equally creepy to leap out at me.

But the bricks were old and the mortar held them firmly in place. I bravely pressed all around the edges but nothing budged so much as a centimeter. I moved on, turning toward another stack of boxes, almost completing my circuit of the room, when a distinctly cold breeze hit the back of my neck.

Goose-bumps rose and my heartbeat thudded in my ears. I spun to stare at the bricked-up doorway. Nothing looked the least bit different. I reached a hand out toward the source of the chilly draft but couldn't detect anything. The air in the cellar was again as still as a morgue.

I shook off the chill and scurried a bit quickly toward the stairs. Flipping off the light I took the steps in doubles and paused at the top, forcing myself to take a deep breath.

Dolly was talking to a customer and the normalcy of their voices brought me back to reality. Surely the old bricked-in area was completely benign and the freshly dug earth . . . well, there had to be an explanation. I squared my shoulders, flipped off the upper light switch and closed the door as I stepped back into Dolly's shop.

"Digging?" she said, as soon as her customer left and I got the chance to ask about the freshly turned earth. "Hm. Archie may have mentioned a plumbing leak a few weeks ago. The man must have left it unfinished. I suppose I'll have to call him back to repair the mess." She said it as if reminding men to clean up messes was her lot in life.

"There's a bricked up wall, about the size of a doorway," I said. "Any idea where that goes?"

"Oh, that. It's old. Apparently in the Middle Ages there were an entire series of tunnels connecting various places in town—pubs connected to the abbey and such. Easy access for monks that were supposed to live an abstemious life, I suppose."

Secret tunnels and bricked entry ways. Spooky. Next she'd be telling me that Jack the Ripper escaped London to come hide out here.

"As I understand it, the river flooded a lot of the tunnels one year—heavens, must be at least a hundred years ago. Some kind of storm drainage system was built but the town fathers decided it would be safer to block the tunnels. A lot of them were backfilled; some of those farther from the river, like ours, were probably just bricked up." She shrugged it off so casually that I had to believe it wasn't a real concern.

But what about that cold draft of air?

Another customer walked in just then and Dolly's attention was diverted to helping the woman decipher a complex knitting pattern so she could choose the correct amount of yarn for it. When a second woman entered I knew Dolly would be occupied for awhile. I gave a tiny wave and left.

Half a block down I spotted Archie coming toward me. "Hi," I greeted. "I hope your interview went well."

He came to a dead stop, stared at me in puzzlement, nodded curtly.

Stupid me. Couldn't I learn when to stay quiet?

"Dolly mentioned it. She was hoping . . . Well, never mind." I started walking again, leaving him standing on the spot. *Charlie, just stay out of it. You've been asked to investigate a couple of silly things, not to get involved in their business.*

Two doors down from The Knit and Purl was a coffee shop. I stopped in, realizing I'd never paused long enough to eat lunch. I ordered a coffee and eyed the apple tarts in the display case. As the girl behind the counter pulled one out for me I decided to follow a new line of inquiry.

"Wasn't there a thrift shop in this block?"

She pursed her lips, which were coated in an impossible shade of glowing pink. "Yeah, maybe a year ago or so?"

"Did it move somewhere else?"

An older woman stepped forward. "The Alzheimer's Care shop? Yes, it's still around. Just go up to the corner, turn right, next street over."

"Thanks." I finished my dessert and coffee and left a tip at the table.

Louisa had mentioned that the thrift shop had not occupied the space very long and had moved rather abruptly. Perhaps they'd also experienced some scary phenomena.

I found the shop easily enough, with a characteristic window display of gently-used items at bargain prices. Business seemed to be good—at least a dozen women browsed everything from overcoats to paperback books. The staff consisted of women in their retirement years, volunteers filling a few hours of their week and helping a worthy charity at the same time.

At my inquiry, a buxom woman whom I guessed to be in her late sixties stepped forward and introduced herself as Agatha Dunston.

"I'm the shop manager," she said. "American, are you?"

I nodded. "Visiting my aunt here in town. Could we talk for a minute? I'm also trying to help a friend of my aunt's with an unusual problem."

She led the way to the back of the shop, where tables of unsorted donations waited.

"Ask away," she said, "as long as you don't mind my working as we talk." She picked and pulled items with the speed of a pro—books, ladies clothing, men's clothing, knick-knacks—each going into separate stacks.

"This friend owns a shop called The Knit and Purl, and they moved into the shop on the next street over, where your shop used to be."

"Ah, yes, I'd noticed that."

"Did you ever experience anything, uh, unusual in that location?"

She chuckled. "My job consists of 'unusual'," she said, holding up a wide-brimmed straw hat decorated with peacock feathers and golf balls. "You might need to be more specific."

I laughed at the hat and she laughed even harder.

"Okay, I see what you mean." I started over. "The current tenant of the shop has experienced several incidents that are downright eerie." I told her about the inventory of yarn being completely rearranged. "On other occasions, liquids went from hot to cold very quickly. More than one person has suggested these events might even be supernatural. So, I was wondering if something like that might account for your organization deciding to move on short notice."

She smiled and nodded her head and I began to think she was agreeing with my statement, until I noticed that her attention was directed toward a fuzzy stuffed chick she'd taken from one of the donation bags.

"Oh, no. I'd not heard of anything strange like that in the old shop. Our decision to move was solely based on the offer of free rent in this spot. A benefactor owns the building and said we could use it. Couldn't say no to that, now could I?"

"No, I don't see how." I fingered the fabric on a turquoise silk blouse she'd just laid in the women's clothing pile. "And you can't think of anything happening that might hint at the shop being haunted?"

Agatha dropped two more blouses onto the stack. "Not really. Well, there was one odd thing. Several times I'd be working in the cellar. It's where I did the sorting. Felt cold drafts a lot down there. Took to wearing my jacket while I worked."

Well, at least my experience wasn't imaginary. I thanked her, picked up the turquoise blouse and held it against myself. It looked to be just the right size. "How much for this?"

She considered for a moment. "Let's say four pounds?"

"I'll take it." I browsed the paperback books on my way to the register, chose two, and tucked my bagged purchases under my arm as I left.

Three unexplained incidents, no answers. I began to feel a little at a loss as to where to turn next. A glance at my watch told me that the day was sneaking by and it was probably time for Louisa to be home from work. I headed toward her place.

I had offered to take her somewhere nice for dinner but Louisa seemed more in the mood for simple food than elegant, so we settled into a corner table at a pub just two blocks from her house.

Over glasses of merlot and a basket of savory bread I filled her in on my adventures of the afternoon.

"It looks like I'm semi-officially hired to find out what's

going on at Dolly's shop."

"Poor dear. Here I had promised you a vacation and now I'm having to work and it looks like you are too."

I shrugged it off. I couldn't ask for a more intriguing assignment, after all. At least no one was shooting at me or whacking me over the head. I mentally erased those thoughts—nothing like inviting trouble.

"Meanwhile, I'm out of ideas on this," I told her. "Ghost hunting is a whole new field to me. Any suggestions?"

She dipped the corner of her bread in the small bowl of olive oil. "You might look up the Trahorn Building—that's what it's called—see if it has past reports of paranormal phenomena. If it does, I'm not aware of it. Of course, I've principally studied the places on my tour route. I guess you'd call them the celebrity ghosts of the town. That's not to say there aren't others. The entire region has a wealth of supernatural activity."

She caught my vacant expression.

"There's a good museum," she said, "Manned by volunteer docents for the most part, but the curator is quite knowledgeable on town history. The newspaper might be another source. It's been in print for ages. Over the years they've probably covered every strange occurrence of any note. You might find a story on the location."

I filed the information in the back of my mind while we finished off a meal of delicately sauced fish and tender vegetables. On the short walk back to her home, Louisa remembered a resource book. As soon as we'd settled in the parlor with mugs of tea she pulled it from her shelf.

"This is a good one," she said, handing me the large hardcover volume. "It covers Bury's history in detail—more than you might want for a light evening read. But somewhere back here . . ." She flipped pages. "There is a chapter about the haunted sites. And further on is a chapter about several heinous crimes, way back in time."

Just what I needed for relaxing bedtime entertainment. I curled into a corner of the sofa with the book across my lap. At some point I became vaguely aware that she'd cleared away the empty cups, said good night and climbed the stairs.

The old house had its own set of noises and I soon switched out the lamp and went upstairs myself, taking the big book along to read in bed. It turned out that there were so many tales of murder, mayhem and ghostly visits that I kept turning pages avidly, completely losing track of time. When the clock downstairs chimed two o'clock I realized that I would never memorize all the names and really didn't need to. All I was accomplishing was to fill my head with gruesome details. I rolled over and let the book lie on the comforter beside me after I switched out my light.

Chapter 9

My late hours spent in the book of hauntings caused me to sleep until nearly ten in the morning and I found that Louisa had left for work much earlier. A note on the kitchen table invited me to help myself to whatever breakfast I wanted and suggested that we might want to try The Fox Inn for dinner. "Save some room—it's fabulous!" she'd noted. She'd also sketched me a little map to show where to find the museum and the newspaper office.

And so it was that I found myself in the other-world atmosphere of a newspaper archive that went back a hundred and fifty years. Luckily, I didn't have to go back quite that far to locate a couple of stories about the Trahorn Building. Background on the more sensational piece informed me that it was built in 1793 in the days of the cattle market. A photo showed it as it looked in the 1800s, with two shops side-by-side—butcher shop on the left, double doors to the slaughter house on the right. A second photo of the location was taken in 1946 with a report of the murder of a homeless man.

By that time the two halves of the building had become individual retail shops, one selling bicycles and the other non-specific one was called Watson and Sons. I puzzled over the photos, trying to place them in modern context. The stone façade above the second floor was the same in 1946 as now, although now it was painted white. Wood trim had been added alongside the display windows, each half done in a different style and color, which explained why I hadn't realized the two shops were actually part of the same structure.

The former bicycle shop was now home to The Knit and Purl. I would have to go back and take a look to see what Watson and Sons had become. Obviously, my powers of observation could stand a little fine tuning.

An elderly man shuffled into the room where the office clerk had parked me with the index to articles.

"One day we shall get all this transferred to microfiche," he said, stepping around me to reach for a file box. "Got the modern bits catalogued already, but it's those historic archives—huge job."

"Am I in your way?" I shifted my chair in hopes that he wasn't about to drop the heavy carton on my head.

"Oh, no. You're fine. I see you've got some pieces on the death of that poor man in the cycle shop. That was a tragedy. Poor chap was sleeping in the doorway, freezing cold night it was. Someone nicked his wallet but had to bash him in the head to do it. Couldn't be content just to take the cash. And him a war veteran and all."

I'd already scanned the article, which didn't mention the weather or the fact that the man was a veteran. "You remember the incident personally, don't you?"

"Aye, Miss. I've covered the news in this town going on seventy years now."

"Can you tell me something? Have there been stories of, say, ghosts or apparitions in the Trahorn Building?"

He set down the carton he'd been holding and bit at his lower lip as he gave the question some consideration. Finally he shook his head.

"No. Not in that one. Now the Cupola House—that one's got a hundred stories. People still claiming to see things there. But the two are a few blocks apart. Why d'you ask?"

I told him that my aunt was a friend of the current tenants, Dolly and Archie Jones. I didn't go into details about Dolly's claims. Talking rumor with a newsman didn't seem like a great idea.

"Archie Jones? He and the wife are living there now? Well, I'll be. Remember one time I covered a ribbon cutting at the sugar mill—this would be maybe ten years ago. Jones was a manager then. Braggart sort of fellow, tall, sort of stiff in the spine, insisted on taking me all round, wanted me to do a big spread on the success of his department. Course we didn't have the space for that. He was none too pleased with me, but I couldn't give in to the man. Hard news trumps a business story. They were lucky to rate a photo and a caption."

I thought of Archie as I'd seen him, somewhat stooped in posture, quiet. A shadow of what this man was describing.

"I could locate the piece for you if you'd like," he said.

"Oh, no, don't go to the trouble. I was just interested in the supernatural history, if there was one."

He picked up the box he'd originally come for. "All right then. All I know's what I've told you, but you might try the museum. Talk to Gertrude Hutchins. Tell her Billy Williams sent you."

And so I did. Mrs. Hutchins was no spring chicken herself, but she was probably a good twenty years younger than Billy. Her eyebrows wrinkled when I told her he'd sent me.

"Surprised he'd want my opinion," she said as she led me into a display room. "We've not shared the same view on anything in thirty years."

Maybe as a newsman he was giving me the chance to get both sides of the story? I simply shrugged and followed her.

"I'm specifically wondering whether there is a history of hauntings or supernatural activity in the Trahorn Building," I said.

Gertrude paused in the center of the room, her gaze darting among the many enlarged photographs on the walls. Her eyes squinted nearly shut and then she turned to her right and headed purposefully into a second room.

"It was in the cattle market section of town way back," she said, pointing to a poster-sized blowup of the same photo I'd seen in the newspaper. "Always something strange in that place."

The descriptive placard under the photo merely said: Trahorn Building, constructed 1793. The Watson Brothers Butcher Shoppe occupied the building until the 1850s.

The grainy photo had to have been taken near the end

of that particular occupancy.

"Sightings of ghostly shapes and horrid noises during the night is what caused the Watsons to close up shop and leave town," my guide was saying.

The spirits of all those butchered cows? "Really? Mr. Williams said there'd never been anything supernatural about the building."

She gave me a pointed stare, reinforcing the comment she'd made about the two of them disagreeing on nearly everything.

"My own great-grandmother was a Watson. These stories have been in my family for generations. My father wouldn't even enter the bicycle shop that moved there in later years. Claimed he'd never trust the work performed under those conditions. In fact, a man on our lane bought a bicycle there and the thing came apart the first day he brought it home. Broke his leg." She ended with a curt nod, daring me to make any statement to the contrary.

I stared again at the photo, as if some faint ghostly image might appear to me. But nothing did.

"Anyhow, take your time and look around," she said. "I'd best get back to my desk."

I made the circuit of the two rooms. One display covered the two most notorious grisly murders of the county's history, including a human skull that purported to be that of a serial killer executed in 1860. After awhile I noticed that the names of the sites were starting to feel familiar to me, but I still hadn't found much that could specifically tie in with Dolly Jones's current problem.

I decided to grab another of those Cornish pasties for an early lunch, this time the chicken and mushroom one Louisa had told me about. I carried it to the Abbey Gardens once again and let the ambiance of flowering beds and birdsong relax me. Before I lost track of all the new information I'd studied this morning, though, I decided to pay another visit to Dolly's shop and report the small scraps of information I'd gained.

Archie looked up from the sales counter when I walked in. At my inquiry he said Dolly was upstairs asleep.

"Poor dear, she hardly slept a wink last night," he said.

I heard footsteps from the stock room and Gabrielle emerged, her face slightly flushed, two knitted throws bundled in her arms.

"Brought these from the cellar," she said to Archie. "Shall I arrange them for display?"

He looked like he would have turned to Dolly for an opinion but since she wasn't there he just nodded.

"Well, tell her I stopped by," I said. I shouldn't wake her for the minuscule amount of information I'd learned.

"It was another of those ghostly things," he said. "The reason she had no sleep."

I'd turned toward the door but I stepped back to the counter. "When did that happen?"

"About midnight. She said she heard a noise down here in the shop. Myself, I slept through that part of it. Woke when she came clattering up the stairs, all shaken up."

"What happened?"

"*Claims* she saw a person here in the shop. When she shouted out, he just vanished. Whoof! Right into thin air."

"You don't believe her?"

"Well, it's just, you know. I never heard or saw a thing. After she come running into the apartment, shoutin' and all, I came down here to check it out. Didn't see a bloody thing."

I glanced around the small shop space.

"Door was locked tight. Only thing out of place was this bin." He indicated a plastic trash receptacle beside the counter. "And Dolly herself admitted she'd bumped into that and knocked it over."

"What do you think she saw?"

He shrugged. "Might be anything. Lights from the street lamps, shadows from the trees."

I turned. "Gabrielle, do you have any ideas what she might have seen?"

The young woman merely shook her head and went back to draping the afghans over a display rack.

"Any rate, Dolly didn't get another wink all night so she asked if I'd take the shop for the morning. She'll be waking any time now. I can check, see if she wants to come down."

I started to tell him not to bother her, but he'd left the room. Besides, it might be good for me to get Dolly's version of events while it was still fresh in her mind. I watched Gabrielle fiddle with the yarns in their racks, seemingly making busy work. She avoided eye contact. In a couple of minutes I heard voices from the back room.

"Charlie? Come on upstairs," Dolly called.

Archie stepped back into the store. "She just got up. In her robe, but she wants to see you."

I closed their apartment door behind me, following small sounds to where I found Dolly in the kitchen, pouring herself a cup of coffee. She held the pot out but I declined.

"Archie said you had a real scare last night," I said.

Something had shaken the woman. Her face was pale and dark circles ringed her eyes. Tangles knotted her normally precise pageboy and the robe hung lopsidedly with the fabric belt undone. Her hands were trembling so badly that she set her mug down.

"It was so real. Then it was completely gone." She sank into a chair at the kitchen table and raked her hands through her hair. "Sometimes I think I'm losing my mind." Her voice broke when she admitted that last part.

I took the other chair. "Start at the beginning and tell me all of it. Exactly what you saw and heard."

She reached for the mug and took two long sips. "Arch and I were sound asleep. Not a thing out of the ordinary that evening. We'd watched a television program then went to bed." Another sip. "I woke to a noise. Very distinct. A thump downstairs. After a few seconds, a second thump. I pictured someone down there messing with the stock again so I grabbed up my robe and rushed to the stairs."

Her hand started to shake again. She set her mug down and took a deep breath, staring at a place in the middle of the table.

"I reached that spot where a person comes out of the stock room, just behind the sales counter. Looked toward the front of the shop. A man stood there, clear as day. I shouted 'Hey!' wanting to scare him away from my yarns."

She looked up and locked eye contact with me. "He let out a long moan, then it was as if he turned to smoke. A dark wisp, gone."

I have to admit that a chill passed through me at the intensity in her eyes.

"When you saw him clearly," I asked, "what did he look like? How tall? What was he wearing?"

She closed her eyes for a second, remembering. "It was dark. His silhouette was framed against the light outside the windows, though. He stood a bit shorter than me, but not much. He wasn't a young lad. It was a grown man. His clothing seemed old fashioned somehow. A cap, and a coat that went almost to his knees."

"How long did you see him like that? Minutes? Seconds?"

"A few seconds at most. The moment I shouted out at him was when he disappeared." She clasped her hands together, as if they would hold each other still. "The thing that frustrates me most is that Arch doesn't believe me. I *know* what I saw."

I had no idea what to make of the information. Her description didn't exactly match anything I'd read or heard about other ghosts around town. It certainly wasn't the Brown Monk or the Grey Lady. I reached out and patted her hand.

"I'd best get dressed and see to the shop," she said. She stood up and carried her mug to the sink.

I told her I would talk to her later. The few scraps of local lore I'd discovered this morning didn't exactly shed any light on this new event.

Down in the shop, Gabrielle handed Archie a heavy carton and he began heading toward the stock room with it. I raised my eyebrows and he paused.

"My opinion?" he whispered. "We watched an old movie last night, black and white, with lots of foggy Victorian scenes. I think she had a dream about it and then walked in her sleep."

He kept moving toward the stock room and I said a quick goodbye, then left.

Maybe Archie was right. My own inclination, had I been in the situation, would have been to believe I'd been dreaming but Dolly was obviously convinced that this had really happened. Suddenly, I didn't know what to think.

A short beep-beep grabbed my attention and I realized I'd stepped off the curb and almost into a tiny car's path. I gave an embarrassed wave to the driver as I moved out of his way.

One of my primary tenets of life is that when things get confusing one should give oneself a treat. I spotted an ice cream shop near the Angel Hotel and popped right in there. On the wall a chalkboard menu listed a bunch of items by names I'd never heard of.

"What's the Knickerbocker Glory?" I asked the teen girl behind the counter.

She held up a tall sundae glass. "We put some fresh fruit in the bottom of this—cherries, peaches, strawberries, kiwi, blackberries and raspberries. Then it's strawberry, vanilla and chocolate ice cream, a scoop of each. Then chocolate sauce, strawberry sauce, whipped cream and a cherry on top. Oh, and it's served with a wafer." She added the mention of the wafer as if I might not be quite satisfied by all the rest.

I felt myself salivating but remembered that Louisa had said to save room for a good dinner. I settled for a small ice cream bar on a stick, making note that I must come back before the end of my stay and have that other glorious concoction.

Despite my little snack I found my energy lagging as I walked up Abbeygate Street. A short rest might help renew me and put all the information I'd learned in some kind of order. I let myself into Louisa's house and settled on my bed with the book of haunted places she'd given me last night.

I must have dozed off within minutes of opening the book because the next thing I knew my eyes flew open when I heard a sound downstairs. Not quite sure whether I'd dreamed it or not, I got up to check out the noise. There at the foot of the stairs stood a semi-transparent figure—a young boy in old fashioned clothing.

Chapter 10

Charlie! Charlie, wake up!" Louisa shook me gently.
I rolled away from the hand on my shoulder and felt the firm binding of the book against my ribs. My heart pounded.

"You must have had quite a bad dream," she said. "You gave out a little shriek."

I shook off the cobwebs of sleep, working to get my eyes focused and my heart to slow down as I stood.

"I came home about an hour ago," she said. "You were sleeping so I tried to be quiet."

"Too much input," I joked. I repeated Dolly's story of the vision she'd had in the night. "Obviously my brain incorporated all of it—the stories from this book and pictures I saw at the museum, along with her mysterious visitor."

She eyed me skeptically.

"Obviously, Archie's comment that Dolly had dreamed the whole thing stuck with me, and I proceeded to dream it myself."

She couldn't very well argue in favor of there really being a supernatural explanation this time. She'd been home and knew that I had not started down the stairs nor had I seen any ghostly person there.

"What time is it?" I asked, noticing that the room was in deep shadow. "Could we declare it happy hour yet?"

"Shall we head for the Fox Inn and have our drinks there?"

I washed my face and brushed my hair then carried the book down to place it back on the shelf in the parlor. Enough of the haunted places research for awhile.

"It's close to a mile each direction," she said as we put on our jackets. "We could take the car if you'd rather not do that much walking."

"The walk will be good for me. Have to shake off the weirdness of that dream."

Softly glowing street lamps gave the street a peaceful ambiance. We cut through the main shopping district where all the stores were now closed and the pedestrian walkways deserted and quiet.

"I love this part of town after dark," Louisa said. "It's so much hustle-bustle during the day but I have the whole place to myself in the evenings."

I agreed that it felt entirely different now. Brightly lit restaurants were filled, obviously the places where many of those pedestrians retired at dinner time. We came to the Fox Inn much more quickly than I expected and were ushered into a nice dining room with heavy wood paneling, high ceilings and white tablecloths.

"How was your day, aside from trying to figure out what disturbed Dolly's sleep?" she asked, once we'd ordered glasses of wine. When it arrived we drank a little toast to staying sane.

"Well, I visited the museum and the newspaper, as you'd suggested. Did you know that the Trahorn Building where Dolly's shop stands was once a slaughter house and butcher shop? In later years it was a bicycle shop." At her smile, I realized what a silly question that was for a local person. "Of course you knew it, didn't you?"

"I'd actually forgotten. My research focused on the high points that would interest tourists. I could probably stand to go back to my books for a refresher on a lot of the other history."

Our server approached to tell us that the special was a lovely portion of prime rib, served with potatoes and vegetables. Somehow I couldn't bring myself to have it, still thinking of the knit shop being haunted by the spirits of all those dead cows. Silly, I know, but I ordered the chicken instead.

"All right," Louisa said once we'd received our starters. "Let's say Dolly really did dream the vision of the man in her shop last night. She obviously didn't dream that her yarns were all scrambled or that the tea scalded her hand. What do you suppose happened on those occasions?"

"The thought came to me that someone is trying to scare her into moving out of the building. But how are they doing it, and why? I have to figure that out."

"The thrift shop folks moved quite suddenly as well. It could be the same thing."

"I checked on that. The manager told me that they'd

received an offer of free rent in their new location. That's the reason they moved, pure and simple."

She pursed her mouth and pushed away her plate. I was still working on my mushroom caps but a new idea occurred to me.

"On the chance that someone may be coming back to look for something, I explored the cellar of Dolly's shop yesterday. I found evidence of digging in the dirt under the stone flooring. She thought Archie had called a plumber awhile back. But what if he didn't? She could be mistaken and someone else left the flooring in a mess."

"Oh, my! A buried treasure or something? How exciting!"

"A bricked-up section of wall was another unusual thing," I said. "When I asked about that she said there used to be a series of tunnels under the town. She assumed the doorway was part of that."

Our entrées arrived then and I could tell that Louisa could hardly wait for our server to leave again.

"The part about the tunnels is true. The river flooded some and the town council voted to fill them in." Her eyes grew bright. "But all that happened quite a way from Dolly's part of town. I seriously doubt her shop was part of the network."

"So what would that bricked-up doorway lead to?"

"What, indeed," she mused.

I cut into my chicken breast. It was incredibly tender and the sauce was perfect.

"Charlie, I think we should offer to stay the night in the shop and see if we can catch the ghost!"

"What?"

"Something or someone is trying to frighten Dolly away. Maybe we can frighten them away instead. It would save her business." With her blond curls and those bright blue eyes she looked like a kid on Christmas Eve.

"I don't know . . ."

"If we caught someone in the act we'd call the police, immediately."

And if we found something valuable down there . . . well, I have to admit to being a sucker for a good treasure hunt. Having devoured all those stories as a kid, a momentary vision of a chest of gold coins or a big pile of jewelry popped into my head.

"We might at least get a look at whoever's coming into the shop and messing things up," I said, practicality taking over again. "If we could stop them it would mean peace of mind for Dolly."

And I could continue my relaxing vacation instead of feeling like I was working. I wouldn't complain about that.

"I'll call Dolly the minute we get home tonight," she said.

We shared a slice of cheesecake and I picked up the check.

* * *

Wednesday afternoon found Louisa and me rummaging through the closet-sized garden shed at the back of her house. She'd spoken to Dolly and our offer to stay the night in the shop had been eagerly accepted. I got the feeling that Dolly would love to hand the whole mess over to anyone, rather than deal with it herself.

"Here's a decent spade," Louisa said, handing the short-handled implement out to me. "Hold on, I think I have another."

I took each tool and set it on the ground. I had my doubts about the whole venture but Louisa had talked a volunteer into taking half of her shift at the office so she could prepare.

We'd decided that taking a few tools along would be smart. I wanted to dig around in that loose earth, just to see if there was more to the story than a simple water leak. And of course Louisa was convinced that a pry-bar would get us through the brick wall and into the realm of the unknown parts of Bury St. Edmonds. She handed one over her shoulder and I took it.

"What about a pail? It could come in handy." She backed out of the small doorway and added a plastic bucket to the growing collection. "There. That should handle things, don't you think?"

We put the bucket and tools into the back of her car.

"We'll park around the corner," she explained, "so the ghost won't see it and realize we're keeping watch."

Uh-huh. I kind of didn't think that was going to be a consideration, but we could do it that way.

Louisa had her practical side, too. At her suggestion we closed our bedroom drapes and took long naps to prepare for staying awake all night. My nap was fitful so I got up and tried phoning Drake, thinking I might catch him before he left for the airport and his helicopter job, but there was no answer on the home phone. His cell went immediately to voicemail, which probably meant he was airborne already and had it switched off. I left a longing-filled message to let him know how much I missed him and how frustrating it was to be on separate continents with all those time zones between us.

Louisa picked up a tote bag and suggested we stop by the market stalls for food.

Although we'd missed the prime morning hours, there were still plenty of goodies to be found. While I gawked at the variety on offer—everything from tulip bulbs to gourmet dog food to books and winter jackets—Louisa gathered bread, cheese, fruit and cookies to go along with the tea she'd packed into a thermos. We would have no excuse for leaving our post.

When The Knit and Purl closed at five o'clock we were watching from the corner. Gabrielle emerged, swinging her purse by its strap as her bouncy steps carried her down the block. I wondered where she lived—was it within walking distance? Or perhaps she rode the bus from another part of town.

Dolly signaled to us and we grabbed our tools and ducked inside. She pulled a shade over the door and locked up. The room went eerily silent when she turned off the background music.

"Arch and I aren't planning on going anywhere tonight but if we change our minds, I'll be sure we use the other door, the one directly to the apartment."

"Is that one locked now?" I asked. No point in guarding the shop if someone could simply get up to the apartment by another means.

She assured me that it was.

I glanced toward the shop-front windows.

"Those remain uncovered at night. And there's a small lamp which stays lit." She indicated the one.

I could see how an intruder wouldn't necessarily be afraid

of being seen. The light might have been all of four watts, barely the size of a Christmas bulb, and the lampshade was a dark parchment color.

"I'm afraid there's no comfortable furniture in here, only my desk chair," Dolly was saying. "But feel free to borrow others from the cellar. Bring something up if you'd like."

"We thought we might spend some time down there anyway," I said with a nod toward the tools. "Checking out that freshly dug spot and all."

She nodded. "Well then, I'll leave you to it."

We were standing in the stockroom at the back of the shop and she turned to head toward the stairs leading up to their apartment. "I've not told Archie about your being here tonight," she said. "Didn't really seem his concern, you know."

"Does that mean we have to stay silent all night?" I asked. "I mean, I wouldn't want him to hear a sound and come down with a pistol aimed at me."

She laughed softly. "That's not a problem. For one, he doesn't own a pistol. And he's half deaf once he takes off his hearing aids at night. Once the telly goes on, he'd not hear a bomb down here."

That was only faintly reassuring.

We bade her goodnight and heard her reach the top landing, go into the apartment, and lock the upper door behind her. The deadbolt had a distinct squeal and I felt sure we would hear Archie coming well before he heard us.

I turned to Louisa. Her eyes were eager, her mouth fixed in an impish grin.

"Well then, shall we settle in?" she asked.

I stood in the doorway between stockroom and shop for a moment, getting the feel of the after-dark place, memorizing the shapes of shelving and merchandise, fixing the images in my mind so I could tell at a glance if anything was later out of place.

"Okay, let's go," I said.

Since it was doubtful that the intruder—human or ghostly—would put in an appearance in the early evening hours, we'd already decided to spend our time in the cellar first. Plus, as Dolly had now mentioned, the sounds of the television upstairs would mask any of our noises as far as Archie was concerned. I still wasn't clear on exactly why she wouldn't simply tell him we were here, but that was her choice.

Louisa took the long-handled shovel, while I picked up the bucket that held all the smaller tools. The cellar looked no different at night than it had when I'd seen it midday, but that was no surprise. I showed Louisa the two odd places I'd discovered.

"I'll have a go at the brick wall," she said, reaching into the bucket for the pry-bar and a hammer.

That left me with that enticing patch of loose earth so I took up the short garden spade.

A few taps at the wall and Louisa was already becoming discouraged. "This thing feels solid as a mountain."

I'd barely turned two shovels of dirt but I set it aside and walked over to where she stood. Even though I'd told her that the bricks looked pretty solid, she'd apparently believed that she would just stick the pry-bar in and start pulling them away.

"Did you knock around on it and listen for hollow places?" I asked.

She took up the hammer and proceeded to hit at the bricks, lightly at first then a bit harder. Each tap brought back only a solid *snick*. No enticing reverberation at all.

"Do you want me to try it, or just keep going?"

"Oh, I'll keep going for a bit. It could be along here somewhere . . ." She kept up the tapping.

For good measure I climbed the stairs to the shop level and then on to the apartment above. Television music from some type of action-adventure show blared loudly enough to reassure me that Archie couldn't possibly hear the little *tink-tink* of our futile mining efforts below.

Back in the cellar again I took up my spade and began to lift shovels-full of dirt into the plastic bucket. The earth on top was loose, almost crumbly, which fit with what Dolly had told me about the recent workman's visit. The puzzling thing was that I didn't see any water pipes or much dampness. Perhaps they'd started this as a test hole and discovered that they really needed to be working elsewhere. I kept going until I'd reached a depth of about six inches spanning the entire two-foot square opening. The small plastic garden bucket had long since filled up and I'd begun piling the shoveled dirt onto the stone flooring beside the hole.

One more scoop or so and then I would tell Louisa it was time to move on to something more productive. But when the tip of my spade went into the ground the next time I heard a distinct *clank*.

Chapter 11

"Whoa!" The word popped out before I'd even lifted the spade. "What's this?"

Louisa rushed over, hammer still in hand, and stared down at the square of freshly turned earth.

I raised the spade again and jammed the blade of it into the dirt. The clanking sound came louder this time. Metallic, like I'd hit a large iron box. I moved the spade around, testing. The metal object was nearly as big as the hole I'd been digging.

"Let's see, let's see it!" Louisa urged.

I scraped at the remaining thin layer of dirt, then we both dropped to our knees and began wiping it away with our hands. Sure enough, there was a round metal object beneath. I felt some raised areas, like an insignia or lettering.

"Get that flashlight we brought," I said, brushing like crazy at the dirt.

Louisa came back with the light and aimed it at the floor. "Drat," she said.

I was still sweeping with my hands, clearing the metal surface.

"Don't bother," she said. "See the wording?"

I could make out B. ST. EDMS MUNI.

"It's an access for the water works. Like a manhole cover."

"What's it doing under a building?" I demanded, miffed that my treasure was turning out to be nothing.

"Who knows? This town has been under construction for a thousand years or more. There are probably water and gas lines running every which way."

My sense of neatness could not fathom such a plan but I had to accept it. Obviously, Dolly's guess that the dug-up earth had something to do with a water leak must have been correct. My treasure chest was a goner.

I heaved a sigh and began to shovel the dirt back over the space.

Louisa stood back, a little dejected that her tapping efforts hadn't yielded anything either. When I'd covered the hole as neatly as possible I glanced at my watch. It was nearly ten.

"I hate to say this, but I think we'd better quit making noises until we can be sure they've fallen asleep upstairs."

"I guess you're right," she said. "This wasn't nearly as much fun as the tombs of Egypt, I must say."

We set the tools aside. I walked up the stairs to the shop level and took a look around. The tiny night light did nothing more than illuminate the top of the table on which it sat, but ambient light from the street showed the familiar shapes of the merchandise and nothing more. For good measure I walked through the shop and shined the flashlight into the darker corners. Nothing appeared out of place.

In the stock room, Louisa had poked around in our tote bag of goodies and she brought out the bread and cheese for dinner, plus the thermos of tea and packet of cookies. We carried them down to the cellar in order to stay as quiet as possible and made ourselves at home on the long leather sofa.

"Okay, I have to ask. *What* tombs of Egypt?"

She gave a half-shrug. "Oh, just another little ghost hunt. I was twenty-seven and someone mentioned a dig. I got all my shots, grabbed up my pack and went along."

"And?"

"Didn't find a ghost. But the place was loaded with urns and gold jewelry and such. Paintings all over the walls. You know."

Well, I didn't *exactly* know but I got a pretty vivid picture. I could see a young Louisa trooping along behind an archaeology team, pestering them the way I'd pestered a certain detective with the Albuquerque police back home. I was beginning to see a lot of myself in her.

She gave me a lopsided smile, along with another wedge of cheese.

"There has to be something here," I said, turning my attention back to the present. "There's a reason someone wants to scare Dolly out of this shop."

But a glance around the cellar full of furniture told me that searching nooks and crannies was probably futile. How would we ever discover just which section of the rock walls or which portion of stone flooring hid the object the intruder was seeking? Unless the cartons and furniture were all removed and we had a way to see the space as a whole, we could spend weeks poking around in here.

When I voiced those thoughts to Louisa she gave a little smile.

"Spirits don't need treasures," she said. "They may want Dolly out of the shop for another reason."

I had no comeback for that, so I offered to check on things upstairs.

As quietly as possible I climbed the stairs to the apartment, walking near the edges of the wooden steps and hoping a loud squeak wouldn't give me away. At the top, all was silent, the television set apparently shut off for the evening. If we allowed the residents an hour or so to fall soundly asleep we could probably resume our search. Meanwhile, I decided to post myself where I could keep an eye on the shop from the dark shadows.

Staying still and quiet while doing nothing is harder than you'd think. Within an hour I felt myself nodding. The whole idea of watching for paranormal activity had begun to grate on me. Whether the incidents had been caused by spirits or people, they were smart enough to stay away while someone kept guard, that was for sure.

I wandered back down to the cellar where I found Louisa running her fingers over a section of the rock wall at the back of the building.

"Finding anything?" I asked.

"Come here and feel this. There is a draft of air coming through a very small opening here."

I joined her and examined the area. Sure enough, a crack showed in the mortar between the small rocks. When I held my hand near it I could feel cold air.

"Where do you think it comes from?" I asked.

"No idea. But it seems there would have to be an open space behind it, right?"

Seemed logical to me.

"I think I'll give it go with the hammer," she said.

I doubted that the small household hammer would make much of a dent against a rock wall. "The apartment is right above this wall," I said. "Better try to keep it quiet."

She experimented with a few small taps and I had to admit that the spot immediately beside the tiny crack did seem to resound with a little more reverberation than the rest of the wall. But it would take a sledge hammer and a lot of work to open much of a hole.

With another reminder to her to work quietly I drifted over to the leather sofa, the one soft spot in the room that wasn't stacked with boxes. A woven throw lay there and I stretched out, pulling it over me. Just closing my eyes for a minute, I told myself. Only one minute.

The sofa was comfortable and I soon imagined Drake's arms around me and that we were snuggled together there. Soon his lips were on my neck and I wanted more than just a snuggle. I woke with a moan of frustration.

"Nice dreams?" Louisa asked from the bottom of the stairs.

I blushed in the dim light and tossed the woven cover aside.

"I went up to the shop for a look around again. Didn't see anything," she said. "Brought sodas and some crisps back with me."

The can of cola gave me a slight energy burst but by the time I'd finished it I also needed a bathroom break. I went up to use the one just off the stock room, took a peek through the shop and came to a dead stop.

I could see the outline of someone standing at the door. There was a small metallic rattle as he tried the knob. I grabbed up the long flashlight I'd left in the stock room earlier and dashed for the door. Hitting the button and reaching for the window shade at the door at the same moment, I aimed the light to hit the person right in the eyes.

But when the shade rose no one was there.

I fiddled with the lock for a moment and flung the door open. The step was vacant. Quick glances left and right. At the corner, about four doors away a man strolled with his back to me, swinging a nightstick and wearing the distinctive cap of a police officer.

I backed into the shop and closed the door as quietly as I could. When I turned around Louisa stood about a foot behind me.

"What happened?" she whispered.

I told her about the cop testing to see that the door was secure, then moving on. "Do you think I made enough noise to wake Dolly?"

"No, you were pretty quiet. What got my attention was when you opened the door. The cold air rushed through the cellar."

"So that crack in the wall does go somewhere," I mused. "It's a large enough opening to draw a decent breeze."

"I guess so."

We made our way back down the stairs as quietly as possible. It was three in the morning.

"Let's take turns resting and watching," I suggested.

With no treasure to be found I just wanted to get this

long night over with. But I didn't want to waste the entire next day sleeping off the adventure. I offered to take the watch since I'd already had a nap, but Louisa was bright-eyed and insisted she wouldn't be able to sleep anyway. I sat in Dolly's desk chair maneuvering to a spot where I could lean back in it and still see the front of the shop without being seen, I hoped, in case the policeman made his rounds again.

At some point I wandered down the cellar stairs to find Louisa asleep on the sofa so I left her there. Eventually, the sky lightened and I began to hear sounds of movement above.

A very long night and nothing to show for it.

I went to fetch Louisa and had to rouse her out of a sound sleep to do so.

"Oh, goodness!" she said. "What time is it?"

"Almost seven."

"I've got work this morning," she said, looking a little frazzled.

"You go on home," I insisted. "I can stay long enough to tell Dolly what we did, just so she doesn't think we vanished, then I'll be along behind you."

She seemed ready to protest my having to stay behind but it only made sense that she get home and have first chance at the shower. She gathered the tools since she was driving and I helped her carry them to her car.

Back in the shop I ran my fingers through my hair and ate two breath mints. I don't think either measure made much difference. The sounds from upstairs were gradually increasing—water running, pots and dishes clanking, the smell of coffee. Above me, the door to the apartment opened.

"No, Arch, don't bother. I'll go down myself," came Dolly's voice.

But she was too late, or he didn't hear her, because he came down the stairs with a zippered bank bag in his hand. He came to a screeching halt when he spotted me.

"Bloody hell!"

"I—"

But I didn't get the explanation out. He took the stairs two at a time and charged into the apartment where Dolly met him at the door. She started explaining and both their voices rose.

I picked up my purse, caught Dolly's glance from the top of the steps, and mouthed goodbye. Even from the middle of the shop I could hear their argument.

"What are you thinking?" he shouted. "An investigator?"

"I want to know—"

"I bloody well will not have it! You'll stop it this instant!"

Her voice dropped. "I can afford—"

But he cut her off with more cursing.

I opened the shop door as silently as possible and closed it behind me. A deep breath of fresh morning air and I started toward Louisa's house. At the corner, the Really Rather Good Coffee House was opening and the aroma pulled me in before I gave it a second thought. Two take-away cups and a small bag with two strawberry pastries found their way into my hands.

Ten minutes later I walked into Louisa's house to the sound of the telephone ringing. No answering machine came on and I debated. I could hear the shower running upstairs. I set the breakfast on the kitchen table and picked up the phone, remembering belatedly that it would probably be either Dolly letting me know that I was fired from my little volunteer stint as investigator, or it would be Archie reading me the riot act.

Luckily, it was neither. "Hey, babe," said Drake's voice.

I was so glad to actually be talking to him that I had to swallow back the emotion that rose in my throat.

"Isn't it the middle of the night there?" I asked after I'd gotten past the I-miss-you-so-much stuff.

"Nearly," he said. "But the time apart is killing me."

"Me too." I confessed to the semi-erotic dream I'd had where I imagined myself snuggled on the sofa with him.

He told me about a dream of his own and we were about to get carried away when I heard Louisa emerge from the upstairs bathroom.

"We'll have to revisit this subject later," I cautioned. I asked about Freckles and about the job he was doing for his demanding customer.

"She's grown some more," he said about the dog. About the job, he told me the money was in the bank and he was glad he'd stayed behind to do the work.

"There's something more," he said. "I've got a job offer in Alaska."

I felt a little whimper escape me. I'd always wanted to go there.

"I'd have to start now. I didn't want to give them an answer until I talked to you."

"How long would you be there?"

"It's recon for seismic work on a potential new oil field. A week or two now, but the main reason I'm leaning toward taking it is that it could easily lead to summer-long work next year. And the pay is very good."

"When?"

"I have to call the guy first thing in the morning with an answer. I'd have to leave Saturday."

"That's in two days! Wh—" My mind raced with all the who-what-where-when.

"You could either join me in Anchorage when you leave England or go on home and I'll get back when I can."

My heart felt pulled three ways. I was loving the visit to Bury. But my commitment to help Dolly was quickly reaching a dead end. I *could* leave earlier than planned. I wanted to be with Drake but what exactly would I do in Alaska? Aside from the obvious making-up-for-lost-time in the bedroom, I'd had no training in seismic work and they were only hiring one pilot at this point, not two. I thought of the long plane flight across the Atlantic followed by another one to reach him. He sensed my wavering.

"Think about it tonight—or I guess that's today where you are," he said. "I'll call you when I have more details. I need to get some sleep now. There's a quick photo shoot on schedule for tomorrow morning and I'll need to spend a full day getting ready to head north."

I sent him a kiss over the line and hung up the phone, a little dazed with the rapidity with which the plans had changed. It wasn't so much that we couldn't handle time apart—his work often required him to be away for days or even weeks. It was just that this felt so *far* away.

Chapter 12

I was standing next to the phone when Louisa came into the room, her hair still a little damp from her shower.

"I thought I heard you talking," she said, with a glance toward the phone.

"Drake called," I said a little absentmindedly.

"All is well at home?" Then she spotted the bag and cups from the coffee shop. "Ooh—you brought breakfast!"

No sense in letting the coffee go cold. I handed one to her and picked up the other. Between bites of the strawberry pastry, she chattered about the night we'd just spent in the Trahorn Building. I could tell she was operating on that particular kind of adrenaline rush that comes with sleep deprivation. She was probably going to crash, right in the middle of her workday.

I envisioned going to bed after she left, hoping for a

couple hours of catch-up sleep, but it was not to be. I'd just finished throwing the cups from our quick coffee into the trash when the phone rang. Hoping that Drake had decided to call back, I dashed for it.

It was Dolly.

"Hi," I said. "Sorry I ran out so quickly this morning. It didn't seem like the right time to hang around."

She cleared her throat. "No problem. Archie and I discussed everything. It's straight now."

I got the impression he was not in the room with her.

"I don't want to cause any problems for you," I said. "I'll just drop—"

"Oh, no. That's not at all why I called. I absolutely want you to keep investigating. I can pay whatever your normal fee is."

"No. I wouldn't want you to do that." Not to mention that I had no idea what complications I could get into by accepting paid work in another country. Better to keep the whole arrangement informal and off the books.

"Would it be convenient for you to drop by sometime this morning? Before eleven, if possible? I'd like to hear how the night went."

I could probably tell her the sum total of it in two words: Nothing happened. But maybe it would be better if I saw her in person. A real conversation might help me sort out the various information I'd found over the past couple of days, as well as getting a better read on Dolly herself.

"I'll try to get there around ten, if that works for you," I said. Before I did anything else at all, I must have a shower.

Later, as I aimed the dryer at my hair, I wondered at Dolly's insistence that I come before eleven o'clock. Were things with Archie really smoothed over, or was she just hiding the fact that she still wanted me around? I found myself alternating between thoughts of her situation and what was going on back at home with Drake's new job. I should probably be booking a flight home rather than poking around in old buildings here. If only I'd figured out how to have myself cloned so I could be in two places at once.

Dolly was alone in the store when I arrived and she had heated the kettle just minutes earlier, so she poured Earl Grey for me in a delicate china cup.

"I feel like I've hit one roadblock after another," I told her after filling her in on the basics of last night's vigil. "Are you sure you want to keep me on the job? I got the impression this morning . . ."

"I do. Even though Archie and I had some words over it." She took a sip from her tea. "I need to know."

"Dolly, there's no physical evidence that someone has been trying to find something hidden in the shop. And I have to admit that the local lore on the history of the place is rather mixed. One person told me the old bike shop had a history, but none of the written accounts back that up. I don't really know where to turn next."

She looked discouraged. "I suppose until something else happens . . . It's just that it never seems to happen when anyone else is around. I feel like I'm the sole target of the incidents."

She pushed her teacup aside. "Charlie, it's not normal for me, feeling so vulnerable."

I remembered my first impression of Dolly, the day we'd met. From the precise cut of her hair to her sometimes abrupt manner of speaking, there'd been nothing fragile or weak about her. Now, after several of these scares, she was looking almost timid. Whatever the explanation, the strain of it was wearing her down.

I took the final sip from my cup and handed it to her.

While she carried the cups to the stock room I glanced again around the shop. After staring at it half the night I didn't expect to see anything different. Only one thing caught my eye this morning. A display rack of cashmere scarves near the door had fallen over, and the scarves were lying in a heap.

"I've still got to put those back," Dolly said, coming up beside me. "I swear, sometimes that man makes me absolutely livid."

She bent down and pulled the wooden rack to its upright position then shook out one of the scarves and draped it attractively over a wooden peg, humming as she worked.

I reached for the doorknob. "I'll keep checking. See if I can learn something new."

But how? I had no experience as a ghost tracker and had certainly found no evidence so far that would tell me how to solve this.

I walked aimlessly to the end of the block and turned right, opposite the way I normally traveled. Maybe I would circle through the old section of town, perhaps even stop in at Louisa's office and brainstorm some ideas if she weren't tied up right then. But before I'd gone three blocks I spotted a police station. Hmm . . . On a whim I entered.

"Is it possible to find records of police reports by address?" I asked the female clerk behind the first desk I came to. Her brass name tag said C. Smith.

Her eyebrows crinkled in a puzzled expression.

I decided to tell almost the whole truth. "A friend owns a shop where there've been some recent small incidents." I didn't dare bring up the paranormal nature of those events. "I'm trying to learn whether anyone filed a police report relating to them."

Anticipating a host of questions, starting with 'Why is this any of your business' I braced myself. But the clerk didn't seem to care. She turned a computer monitor to get a more straight-on view of it.

"How long ago did this happen?" she asked.

"I'm not exactly sure when they began—"

"Within the past twenty-five years?"

I tended to forget that anything within a hundred years around here was considered new history.

"Probably within the last few months," I said.

"Address?"

I'd seen it printed on Dolly's sales receipts and recited the information to her. She clicked a few keys.

"The Trahorn Building. Nothing that recent," Ms Smith said, reading from the monitor. "There was a break-in in 1997 where the tenant reported some merchandise missing. But the investigation revealed that his partner had merely taken the things home for personal use."

"Is that the most recent incident?"

She nodded. "A shoplifting report in 1989 . . . Before that, we'd have to go to the old records section. It's a large, dusty room in the basement."

I couldn't see where anything that old would be relevant to Dolly's current problems, plus I got the distinct idea that the clerk was no more eager to go into the dusty archives than I was.

"No, that's okay," I said. A thought came to me. "What

about personal complaints? Anything under the name of Dolly Jones?"

"The lady with the knit shop?" she asked. "I know of her."

"Really? Personally?"

"Just heard the name, round about, you know." She typed a few more words as she said it. "Um-hmm. All right . . ." A couple more keystrokes. "Here in the telephone logs."

She turned the screen so that I could see it.

"We have to log every call, whether or not there's basis for police action."

I scanned the white letters on their blue background, not making immediate sense of what I was seeing.

"This is the date," Ms Smith explained, pointing to the left-most column of numbers. "Followed by time of day, caller's name, caller's phone number, summary of the complaint. To get the entire text of the complaint, you just hit F1."

I noticed Dolly's name at the top of the page. There were at least ten complaints.

"Mrs. Jones certainly complained quite a few times," I said.

"Oh no," she answered. "These are complaints *against* Mrs. Jones. Notice that the calls all came from others."

Oh boy. I started to read across the lines.

Sally Darcy, clothing store manager. Complaint: Dolly Jones tried to return obviously used merchandise for refund. Caused a scene upon being denied the refund.

James Gilcrist, restaurant owner. Complaint: Mrs. Jones entered his restaurant, carrying a dog. Refused to acknowledge signage warning that no pets were allowed and refused to place the dog on a leash. Set the pet on the floor where it proceeded to do its business in front of other customers. Jones caused a scene when Gilcrist threatened to call police.

Joshua Raintree, plumber. Complaint: Performed work for Mrs. Jones for which she refused to pay, saying the bill was too high despite the fact that he had quoted her the same amount before doing the job.

And on and on.

"Did the police act upon any of these?" I asked.

"Let's see." She turned the monitor a bit and opened another page. "The plumbing contractor was advised to try the small claims court. Most of these charges don't actually violate an ordinance. We usually advise a business owner to try to make private arrangements for reimbursement, if that seems warranted. Most of them won't—they are usually more worried about adverse publicity for their establishments. Unless the subject actually strikes someone or causes physical damage . . ."

"There's nothing you can really do."

"Exactly."

I thanked her and walked back out to the street. This certainly put a whole new spin on things. I'd never quite put two and two together, but when I thought about it I'd not seen many customers in her shop. Maybe Dolly really had few friends and word of her reputation had spread. And maybe one of those who went far enough to make a call to the police had gone even further.

I realized I'd come back to Abbeygate Street and decided that another of those Cornish pasty lunches would be in order. I would have to decide how to proceed, whether I could actually offer any help to Dolly at all, or if it would be best to steer completely clear of her.

An hour later, appetite sated, I gave myself over to a leisurely stroll through the Abbey Gardens. Deep blue skies and sunshine had returned during the morning and I enjoyed walking among the older ruins which dated back to the Middle Ages and reading the placards that showed the old abbey as it would have once stood. It felt like I'd covered miles and a seat on one of the benches beckoned me.

"Poor chap, you have to feel for him," a male voice said, from the next bench over.

"Can't be easy, that's sure, losing the job at his age, being stuck home with the woman all day."

I sent a glance to my right and saw two men in business suits, late forties or early fifties in age, obviously on an afternoon break from work, both spooning ice cream from cups that must have come from the vendor I'd seen outside the gate.

"Ha, especially that one. I'd go packing in a trice."

The other man sighed. "Yeah, poor Arch."

I would have filed the whole conversation away as nothing until he said the name. Archie Jones? The circumstances certainly fit. I realized that I'd turned toward the men and that they'd noticed my unabashed eavesdropping. I covered by noticing a scrap of litter on the ground beside the bench, picking it up and heading for a trash bin with it.

My impressions of Archie had been of a man solicitous of his wife, caring and right there at her side. Was the other side of it perhaps that Dolly tended to push him around, to be a bit too controlling? Why not? It certainly seemed to fit with the way she treated other people in this town.

I climbed three steps built of rocks and ducked through

a narrow opening in a hedge, coming to another section of the garden, this one much closer to the towering Gothic Abbey. Maybe a dose of peace and brotherly love would help settle my mind.

The cloisters, where I found myself entirely alone, provided a little haven. The Gothic arches rose on my right, while a walled rose garden to my left gave the sense of seclusion. I paused to contemplate a stone mandala set in the walkway.

"It's not exactly a work of art, is it?" a male voice said.

I must have jumped three feet. He stood a few yards away, dressed in khaki pants and a checked shirt with a soft-brimmed hat sitting a little crooked on his head. I guessed him to be in his late 70s. Beside him a wheelbarrow held clippings from the bushes. He'd certainly arrived quietly.

"That emblem," he said, nodding toward the object of my attention. "It's not really of high quality."

"I'm not exactly an expert on that type of thing," I said. "Mainly, enjoying a stroll through the gardens."

"It probably dates back to only the seventeenth century or so."

And people are allowed to walk on it? I thought of the ancient abbey ruins in other parts of the garden, where I'd seen children climbing. Aside from one discreet sign advising that defacing the ruins was illegal, apparently the townsfolk believed in accessibility to their history.

He set his shears down in the wheelbarrow and tipped his hat back to wipe his very high forehead.

"You're American, right?"

I laughed. It was pretty obvious, I supposed.

"Enjoying Bury, are you? Have you met any of the town ghosts?"

"I'm visiting my aunt, actually. She gives tours of the haunted sites in town and has promised to take me along on her next one."

"Ah, you'll enjoy it. I've never seen one myself, but my late wife—she was a great believer. Swore that The Grey Lady used to help with little chores around the house. I have my doubts about that part of it. But it seemed to make her happy that she had company whilst she did her work."

I could tell that he was a little eager for company. But when he launched into the third tale of the Abbey's more ethereal inhabitants I knew I would have to say goodbye or I'd never get out of there. I used the excuse that I was meeting someone and would be late.

It was nearly true. After my visit to the police station I'd decided that I should just tell Dolly that I couldn't be of help in her search for the poltergeist in her shop. There were just too many people in town who might have reason to get back at her. How was I going to narrow it down? And what would she do anyway—retaliate by filing a complaint against the perpetrator? I could see the whole spiraling into a quagmire.

I left the Abbey grounds, crossed in front of the Angel Hotel and started up the street toward The Knit and Purl.

The small bells at the door tinkled softly, but Dolly spun around as if she'd been shot. Her eyes were wild and her normally precise hair looked as if she'd been trying to yank it out.

"Charlie!" My name came out in a whoosh. "Look at this! It's happened again!"

I followed her pointing finger to the spot where I stood. There on the floor were large muddy boot prints.

"When—?"

"Just now! I'd taken a moment to visit the ladies room, walked back in here, and *this*!"

Chapter 13

I knelt down. The prints were, indeed, still a bit damp. They appeared to have been made by large feet, with the kind of treads common to hiking boots. They led from the front door to the sales counter. I followed the trail and saw that the prints circled the desk and ended in front of the register.

The cash drawer was standing open. I pointed at it. "They may have taken your money."

She rushed to the spot, her eyes darting back and forth, her hands reaching for the contents. "No, it seems the notes are all here, and the coins . . . But the mess! Look!"

I didn't immediately see what she was getting at.

"Everything's in a jumble," she said. "Look, all the coins are mixed together every which way, pounds and pence together, and the notes look as if they've been shuffled." She picked up a handful.

Sure enough, the multi-colored bills were combined in a bright bunch.

"This drawer was in absolute order not five minutes ago." Her eyes were wide, her voice shaky. "How can this be happening to me?"

Karma? I didn't know what to say.

Her hands shook as she sorted the money back into the proper denominations. One by one she placed the paper money back into the long slots. Then she began on the coins.

I didn't have the heart to tell her my original reason for coming in, to quit investigating her case. While she concentrated on getting the drawer back in order I looked around the room.

Then it hit me. The boot prints went from the front door to the register . . . but they never left. There was no trail back to the door, to the stockroom, or anywhere.

"No one else was in the shop at the time?" I asked.

She shook her head. "Gabrielle comes in at noon on Thursdays. Archie went out early. I was here entirely alone." Her voice shook a little. The idea of being by herself and an intruder showing up clearly had her rattled.

I tried to bring her back to the facts. "Are these prints the same as the ones you mentioned before? Do they look like they were made by the same boots?"

She looked up from her stacks of coins and stared at the prints. "Definitely not. The others were smooth, these have a pattern."

That was at least a firm clue. Either two different people had made the tracks or the prankster was smart enough to wear different footwear each time. Perhaps it was his way of making Dolly believe she had more than one ghost.

"Okay. Take me through it again. You were here by yourself."

She nodded.

"You went into the bathroom."

Another nod.

"You never heard a sound out here? Not the front door bells, not the cash drawer opening, nothing?"

"Not a thing. I couldn't have been in there more than two or three minutes."

"Of course there is the music," I said. "Maybe it drowned out any sounds?"

"I'm very accustomed to the background music," she insisted. "I hear any little noise, even with it playing."

I let it go. Clearly, there was no point in arguing. I was beginning to see her stubborn side. I turned my attention to the physical evidence instead.

The door chime consisted of four small brass bells hanging by a cord from the wooden bar that bisected the door. Motion caused them to clink against the glass inset on the door. I supposed that someone who noticed the bells hanging there could open it cautiously enough that they wouldn't ring.

A low spot on the sidewalk outside tended to hold water—I'd noticed that before and usually just stepped around it. But someone not paying attention or anyone who wanted to leave prints on purpose could step into it and, if their boots already held some dirt, the tracks were easily explained. But how did they get away without leaving a single print in the opposite direction?

That was the question I could not answer.

Dolly, meantime, had arranged the cash drawer to her liking and appeared from the stock room with a sponge mop in hand.

"I'd better get this cleaned up before a customer sees it," she said.

I glanced at my watch, hoping for an excuse to leave. I didn't have any easy answers for Dolly, but thought I would ask Louisa for ideas. I have to admit that I probably scurried away from the knit shop a little abruptly.

Back at Louisa's house I calculated the time difference and decided I might be able to reach Drake at home. He answered on the second ring and we followed our prearranged plan—he called back immediately so we wouldn't run up Louisa's phone bill.

"I contacted that boarding place for Freckles, the one we'd planned to use before," he said. "I'll take her by there this afternoon and make sure everyone gets along fine."

"Should I come home? I feel like I'm not exactly there to help you with all this."

"We talked about that when we first got the puppy, hon. We're on the go a lot. When she can travel along, she will. When it's not feasible she'll learn to stay in a doggy hotel. She'll adapt easily if we start her out young."

He was right of course.

"I did a little research on the company I'll be working for. Good outfit, and my knowing the chief pilot from years ago in Hawaii is a plus. He knows my work and gave a high recommendation to the owner. If I jump through a few hoops now, they'll hire me again next summer and the money for that will be very good. And, you can come along if you want."

A little mental yippee went through me. Missing out on Alaska was the main reason I'd felt the tug to catch up with him this time.

"I can get home early next week and rescue Freckles," I said. "Louisa and I haven't gotten a lot of time together, but there's a weekend coming up for that." I filled him in on how I was spending my days and he chuckled over the fact that I'd latched on to a mystery to solve.

"I'm not a bit surprised," he said. "Things seem to happen wherever you go, my little detective."

We ended the call with a plan to touch base again before he left Albuquerque and a promise that he would keep me posted on his trip.

The front doorknob rattled and Louisa came in, carrying a plastic handled bag.

"Dinner in tonight?" she said, holding it up. "Home cooked, almost."

She carried the bag into the kitchen and pulled out a jar of marinara sauce and the ingredients for salad. From a cupboard came a packet of long spaghetti. She started to apologize but I just laughed.

"You have no idea how close this is to my way of doing things at home," I said. "I would have no clue how to make this from scratch. Drake is a far better cook and actually makes an excellent sauce."

"I had a man like that once. Luigi." She made the name sound almost musical. "He owned a vineyard in Tuscany and his linguine was as luscious as his—" She stopped and cleared her throat. "Too bad I let him go."

I grinned at her but she didn't seem inclined to give more details.

"I can open a bottle of wine," I told her. "If you'll point me toward the corkscrew."

I poured two glasses while she filled a pot with water

and turned on a flame under it.

"Dolly had another scare at the shop today," I said, once we'd settled into our comfy corners on the old sofa in the parlor. I filled her in on the details.

"What on earth could be causing all this?" she mused. "And right after we were there last night."

I let a moment go by. "Have you known Dolly very long?"

She sipped from her glass. "A few years, mainly through the knitting group. Outside of there, I've only run into her a few times around town. It's a small place, but we don't actually see everyone every single day."

"I just wondered whether she has a lot of friends." I told her a little about the reports I'd seen at the police station.

"My, you have been thorough," she said, heading toward the kitchen when the timer on the pasta went off. "She's always been friendly enough with me but I've heard a few things . . . people who don't seem to care much for her, a couple of women who refuse to patronize her store. I'd no idea some had actually made official complaints."

I trailed her into the kitchen where she was in the process of mixing the greens and shaking a vinaigrette dressing onto them. She carried the salad bowl to the table.

"I wonder if her behavior accounts for business at the shop being so slow. Once I thought about it I realized I've rarely seen another customer in there."

"The size of the knitting group certainly dwindled over the summer." Louisa handed me a plate. We dished up the pasta and sauce and took our seats.

"I wonder whether she's made someone mad enough to go to these lengths to scare her. Maybe the idea that someone is trying to frighten her out of her shop isn't so far off. It could just be for other reasons than we'd ever guessed."

We ran the subject around in circles and finally decided we were merely blathering, exhaustion from our sleepless night having taken over our brains. When I noticed Louisa's eyelids drooping I suggested that we call it a night. It was seven o'clock.

I brushed my teeth and thought I would peruse the book of haunted places once more, but even that didn't last very long. I switched out the light within fifteen minutes and fell into a deep sleep.

My next conscious thought came when I began to smell coffee. Slipping on a pair of jeans with my sleep-shirt I padded down the stairs barefoot to find Louisa in the kitchen.

"Sorry. I tried to be quiet," she said. "Lucky thing I'd set my alarm or I would still be off in dreamland somewhere."

When she asked about my plan for the day I had to admit I didn't really have one. It seemed pointless to keep searching out ghosts on behalf of Dolly, even though she'd begged me to keep working on it. I really didn't have any fresh ideas whatsoever.

"I'll be giving my Haunted Bury tour tomorrow night," she reminded me. "If you want to come along I'll put your name on the list. It takes a couple of hours but the total distance to walk is less than a mile."

Why not, I decided. Some fact that she'd forgotten to tell me might come out in the talk.

"Use your time today to rest up," she warned as she was walking out the door. "The tour lasts until midnight." With a spooky little eh-eh-eh she left.

Spending the day lounging around and resting sounded really good but I found myself too keyed up to sit still. Of course the early bedtime and two cups of coffee might explain it. I read the first couple of chapters in one of the books I'd bought at the thrift shop, a mystery in which the psycho killer is the good guy and everyone else in the story is even more messed up.

As the sun warmed the house and it began to creak I decided I'd be better off taking a long walk, and that's when I found myself on Lilac Lane, and *that's* when I realized an ambulance with brightly flashing lights was sitting right in front of The Knit and Purl.

Chapter 14

I froze in place for a full minute. The whole scene felt surreal. From the front door of the knit shop, technicians wheeled a stretcher covered in a white drape. The uneven shape of a body meant this wasn't good news. My feet took off running.

The ambulance's strobes went still and the vehicle pulled away from the curb. A man in a dark suit picked up a black valise from the sidewalk and headed toward a car that I hadn't noticed before. On the side of it, a sign said Coroner.

Archie Jones stood in the shop's doorway, his face white and slack with disbelief. His eyes were dead orbs.

"What happened?" I said, rushing up to him.

His mouth opened, closed, opened again but no sound came out. I stood right in front of him, trying to get his attention.

"Archie! Look at me!"

Gradually, his gaze homed in on my face.

I made my voice slow and gentle. "Archie, what happened?"

"Dolly. They've taken her." His dead-looking eyes began to leak slow trails of tears.

"Let's go inside," I said, stepping forward to steer him into the shop.

Inside, things seemed to be in order. The bins of expensive yarns sat in organized rainbow arrays. The oils and herbs in their tiny bottles rested on the glass shelves, none out of place. The scent of candle wax hung heavy in the air. I led Archie to Dolly's chair behind the sales counter and asked if I could bring him some water. He shook his head.

"Can you tell me what happened?" I asked, kneeling to be at eye level with him.

"That man," he said. "He said there would be an inquest."

"Was there an accident? Did she become ill during the night?"

He shook his head again. "I woke up this morning. She was lying beside me. Cold."

How awful. No wonder the man was in shock. I paced to the front of the shop, unable to stay still. At this point it wasn't really my business, but I couldn't simply walk out and leave the poor man there alone. The couple had no children, I remembered Louisa telling me.

"Is there someone I can call for you?" Surely he had friends, former colleagues.

He continued to stare at a spot in the middle of space.

Okay, now what? I automatically touched the side

pocket of my purse where I normally kept my cell phone but of course it wasn't there. My reflex in times of trouble is usually to call either Drake or Ron, but that option wouldn't accomplish anything here and now. What was the official name of Louisa's workplace? I should phone her.

"She was so upset last night," Archie said in a flat voice. "The candles."

What on earth was he talking about? I glanced around and my gaze fell on the shelves of candles on display. Something didn't look right. I stepped closer and saw that they'd been lit. Every one of them.

"Archie? These candles?" I pointed. "Who lit all these candles?" I pictured Dolly trying some sort of massive exorcism to rid the shop of her ghostly fears.

He shrugged. "We didn't know. We were watching the telly, same as always. Dolly smells the candles. Comments on it a couple of times. I didn't think it was anything. She insists on it—something's wrong, Arch, she said to me."

He'd stood up and walked over to stand near me. "So she comes down from the apartment. They're all lit." He pointed to the candles. "She screams and I come down, and she's got a little tamper thing and she's putting them out. She's screamin' out some choice words, I'll tell you, mad as a hornet that her stock's all ruined."

At least she'd gotten all the flames out before anything else in the store was damaged. I could imagine how upset she'd be, having to order all new stock and then practically give these away since they weren't pristine and new anymore. Maybe the loss would be too much for the small shop that wasn't exactly thriving anyway.

The chimes at the door sounded and Gabrielle popped in, looking perky in a pink sweater that set off her flawless complexion. Her smile faded when she caught sight of Archie's face.

"I'm afraid I've some bad news," he said.

I gave him a light pat on the shoulder and left so he could explain the situation privately. I wondered how Gabrielle would take the news of her sudden unemployment. I'd gotten the impression that working in the yarn shop was more a pastime than a passion for her anyway. She would probably find another job fairly soon.

Meanwhile, speaking of being unemployed, I supposed I was officially off ghost-buster duty for good. I couldn't say I was all that unhappy about it, but the image of the ambulance taking Dolly away from her shop continued to haunt me.

My steps carried me toward the tourism office where Louisa would be on duty this morning. I needed to tell her about Dolly's death before she heard it elsewhere. Undoubtedly eyes all up and down the block had seen the sheeted body and the fact that the coroner's car had been there. I couldn't imagine that the small-town gossip mill wouldn't operate all that differently from what it would in America.

I held back while Louisa finished ringing up a gift shop purchase—three postcards and a mug imprinted with the image of the Abbey. When the patron left I tilted my head toward a closed door.

"Are we alone?" I asked.

Her eyebrows went into a puzzled curve. "Yes, why? What's happened?"

"It's Dolly." I told her what I'd seen and about the subsequent conversation with Archie. "He's absolutely in shock."

Her face paled and her gaze drifted to a spot far away. "Those burning candles. Another unexplained event. Do you think it sent her over the edge?"

"There's no way of knowing. Can a person literally die of fright?" But even as I asked the question I reconsidered. Archie had said Dolly was angry over the candles, not scared. Maybe she'd gotten so worked up that she'd burst a vessel or something. "I guess only the inquest will tell."

* * *

I itched to be doing something all day Friday and Saturday. Louisa called another tourism office volunteer to take her shifts and the two of us basically wasted time shopping and sitting around the house. Drake checked in with me Friday night from a hotel in Anchorage. He would be out at a line camp starting Monday morning. I told him I should at least stay with Louisa until after Dolly's funeral.

The service was set for Monday afternoon, and I could do nothing more than wait around to ask about the results of the inquest.

"Come along on my tour," Louisa insisted on Saturday night. "It's been on the schedule a long time so I have to do it. And it will help take our minds off this other subject."

So, we bundled up in sweaters and scarves. Louisa picked up a roomy shoulder bag and we headed out to meet the tourists at the Abbey Gate at ten p.m. In the glow of lamplight, two teen boys waited. They called out, greeting Louisa by name.

"Groupies," she whispered. "They fancy themselves ghost hunters, but since the Abbey Gardens are closed at night except to us, this is the only way they can hope to come across some of the better-known ethereal residents. Plus, Tim's mother is a friend of mine. She knows she can trust me to keep an eye on the boys so they don't go wandering off or sneaking into someone's home because they think it's okay to wait around for the spirits to show up."

"Mr. Partridge isn't here yet," the taller of the two boys said.

"That's all right. We have six others joining us yet. We'll wait awhile." She introduced the boys to me as Sean and Tim, and the basic difference I could see in them was that Tim was the tall one. Otherwise, they were clones in nearly identical black jeans and T-shirts, with dark knit caps over brown collar-length hair. Their trendy coats looked like Abercrombie to me.

A uniformed man showed up on the other side of the gate and he also greeted Louisa familiarly. This must be Mr. Partridge, the guardian of the gate at night. Sean and Tim both said hello to him.

About that time two couples came walking from the front of the Angel Hotel, just across the road. Obviously American in dress and voice, I learned that they came from Indiana and it was their first trip to England. One of the women seemed to be a fan of television shows about haunted sites and she'd heard of this tour and dragged her husband and friends along.

Louisa consulted a sheet of paper she'd pulled from her pocket and checked off the four names. She glanced up and down the sidewalk, then pulled her sleeve back to check her watch. She seemed satisfied with whatever it told her.

No more than two minutes passed before another couple came hurrying up, a tense conversation in brusque tones taking place between them. They were well bundled in woolens and sturdy shoes and the woman's blond hair was done in a long braid down her back. Louisa looked at her list again. The man looked apologetic. *"Wir sind spät. Traurig."*

"Guten Abend," she said. *"Verstehen Sie Englisch?"*

I stared at my aunt. Where had she learned this?

"Ja, pretty well," the man answered.

"No problem. If you have any questions you may ask me," Louisa said. "Now, group, I think we are all here. Shall we enter the gates?"

I noticed that her voice changed timbre at that phrase 'enter the gates' setting the mood and preparing us for the idea that we were about to get very spooked. Partridge took hold of a chain that ran over a pulley system and pulled. The heavy iron gate began to rise. He paused it about six feet off the ground, a fraction of its total height, and we walked under. Once everyone had cleared the entry, he let it lower with a clang. Wide eyes all around told me that everyone had that same point-of-no-return feeling.

Chapter 15

The ten of us stood in nearly complete darkness under the massive arch of the Abbey Gate, that entry which had felt benignly historic in daylight. Louisa turned to the group and issued a few basic rules.

"We are allowed to enter the Abbey grounds after sunset only with special permission," she began. "Therefore, everyone must stay with me at all times. No exploration on one's own, please, and no walking off the prescribed pathways."

She gave the teens a pointed look, which made me believe this had been an issue in the past.

"I'm handing out small torches—flashlights—to each of you. The paths can be uneven in a few places and parts of the grounds are not well lit."

Again, a stern look at the boys. I pictured them making

scary faces with the lights under their chins or other goofy antics, but since Louisa had the power to kick them off the tour and to tell their mothers, I doubted there would be any problems.

She went into her tour-guide voice. "You probably know some basic history of Bury St. Edmunds and the township. Contrary to popular opinion the name Bury was not meant to convey the fact that St Edmund was buried here, although he was for a time. The place was originally called Beodericsworth More likely, the etymology of this use of the word 'bury' stems from similar words like borough, burg, or borg, which simply mean 'city.' Around the year 906, the king's remains were sent here for burial, later removed to London during the Danish invasion, and later returned once more. Because of the Danish treatment of the monks here at the Abbey, several of them are known to haunt the grounds. It is said that King Edmund's ghost exacted revenge on the Dane, Sweyn Forkbeard, by striking him dead of a heart attack. There are also legends of a missing treasure—a precious gold statue of the archangel Michael—which has never been found."

Tim's and Sean's eyes sparkled at this, although since they'd often been on Louisa's tours, it could have hardly been news to them.

Louisa continued, "Naturally, there have been frequent sightings of the famous Brown Monk right here under *this very gate.*" She paused for effect. "Additionally, during the turbulent 1600s, Bury St. Edmunds was the site of the infamous witch trials and you can imagine how many restless souls remain among us. But tonight we are not here to speak specifically of dead kings and ancient history, except as it might relate to those inhabitants who have *never quite* left this earth."

Again, her tone dropped and she paused between the words to convey the mysterious. I had to give my aunt credit for her delivery skills. She led us from the oppressive overhang of the stone gate onto the central garden pathway where occasional lamp posts cast minimal lighting, throwing the whole scene into a montage of black, gray and dim green. The teens dropped to the back of the group, but I noticed that the four Americans kept close pace with Louisa.

She purposely took the narrowest pathways, leading us between the black hulking shapes of the ancient stone ruins, up a short flight of uneven steps, across lawns that were rapidly becoming thick with dew. I had walked most of this ground during daylight hours but had to admit that the nighttime visit was far more eerie. Every dozen yards or so she would pause to talk about the monks who lived here in ancient times and to let the group catch up with her.

"Watch for the Brown Monk," she cautioned. "He is often seen in and around the grounds of the Abbey."

Before anyone could spend much time in finding him, she'd headed toward the huge building of the cathedral itself. On our right appeared a row of doors set into a massively proportioned three story stone building that seemed part ancient, part relatively new—as new as anything in this town. I guessed only four or five hundred years old.

"These are the Cathedral Cottages," Louisa said quietly, lowering her voice. "They have been converted to modern residences, so we must be considerate of the current occupants."

I noticed that only a few lights shone at windows.

"A monk—many believe him to be the Brown Monk— often pays visits to these homes. Women have reported awakening in the night to find him sitting at the end of their beds. He never makes a move, never says a word. Then he vanishes."

Okay, I have to admit that a little chill went through me at that point. When the German couple moved closer I didn't object to the company.

The group tightened a bit more when Louisa led us into the graveyard. Again, even though I'd been there in daylight, the black mounds of earth seemed larger now. And did that one beyond the big tree actually move a little?

"Here on our left, Saint Mary's Church is the burial place of Queen Mary Tudor, daughter of King Henry the Eighth," she told us. She went into some of the history, and it seemed to me that she lingered a bit long over the queen's famous nickname, Bloody Mary. As we strolled past, she went on with a tale of a clergyman in the 1930s who believed he could contact his long-lost twin through séances. The leap in time was pretty far, and I realized that my mind must have wandered. I found myself thinking of Dolly Jones and how she'd become convinced that something supernatural was happening in her shop.

"... of course the entire story of the Grey Lady was later revealed to be pure fiction, a story written as an historical novella in the 1800s. Even so, there are still people who see things that cannot entirely be explained away."

By this time we had traversed the graveyard, on the path under the heavy overhang of trees, and emerged—thankfully—onto the street. A passing car provided a dose of modern reality and one of the women giggled in nervous reaction to it. Louisa caught my eye, behind the backs of the others and gave me a wink.

"All right, folks. You shouldn't need your torches

anymore," Louisa said. "We will be on lighted streets from this point onward."

Those who had been using them switched them off and Louisa stowed them in her tote bag.

"We next take a look at two well-known landmarks here in Bury. The Dog & Partridge Pub, and then in a few minutes, the Theatre Royal."

Once more, since I'd already been to the pub and walked past the theater on a number of occasions, I found my thoughts focusing on Dolly. I ticked through the incidents in the shop—the mysterious footprints, the admittedly unexplainable fact that tea had gone hot and cold, and the ruined lit candles—which may have been the proverbial straw that sent Dolly beyond sanity.

"Several of these shops on Whiting Street experience regular visitations from the spirit world," Louisa was saying. "Knocking and tapping sounds . . ."

I thought of the night we'd spent in the cellar at Dolly's. How easy it might have been for anyone else in the building to construe our small attempt at digging up what we thought was treasure to be something caused by ghosts. I sent sidelong glances toward my fellow tour-goers, feeling a shot of disdain for their rapt attention and utter belief in things that were so easily explained away. If I could make noise in the cellar of a building, surely anyone could.

"At this next intersection we'll see The Nutshell Pub, Britain's smallest pub and home to a particularly sad ghost, that of a little boy. He has been seen several times in a tiny upstairs room, sitting alone at the table as if waiting for his parents to return for him."

The women looked stricken, and I have to admit that the way Louisa told it, anyone with a heart would have felt sorry for the child. I looked toward the curved glass corner window. The place was quiet, with only a small nightlight illuminating the rich wooden bar and walls.

"Whether or not you are fortunate enough to see the ghost, simply stopping in for a drink and to see the artifacts is well worth your time. Tim and Sean, your drinks will have to be sodas, I'm afraid."

That comment drew a titter from the crowd, but it helped to disperse the gloomy mood over the sad child-ghost.

"Come forward for a moment," Louisa said, leading us up to the glass-fronted building. "It's hard to get full detail in the dim light, but do note the mummified cat hanging from the ceiling. In times past, it was considered prudent to bury a cat within the walls of a building as it was constructed. Cats kept vermin away and acted as a good-luck symbol. No one knows exactly where this particular cat was found or how long it has been hanging here."

I glanced in the window. The walls were papered with currency from many countries in many denominations and there were so many other oddities hanging on the walls that at first I had a hard time spotting the rigid figure or recognizing it as feline. I figured this was one tradition that I could skip if I were ever to build.

"In the next block, the Suffolk Hotel was quite nice in its day. Its history goes back as part of the Abbey property as far as the year 1295, and it was licensed as an inn in 1539." She gave us North Americans a moment to absorb those dates. "But the reports of haunted happenings are much more recent, clear up to the time the hotel was closed in 1996 and converted to shops.

She stopped on the sidewalk and motioned to the large

white building on the opposite side of the street, where I recognized the bookshop and clothing store where I had shopped earlier in the week.

"Couples who met at the hotel for extra-marital trysts were often vulnerable to the pranks of the ghosts. Noises in the rooms were common as soon as the lights went out, but when the light was turned back on again, the rattling would stop. One guest complained to a porter that his lover refused to stay the night. She apparently leaped from the bed, dressed, and fled the property before he was quite . . . um, finished."

A picture of Archie Jones's face came to me. Not the shell-shocked Archie of two days ago, but another version. I shook my head. It didn't make sense. I turned my attention back to Louisa who was on the move once more. We were back on Abbeygate Street in a couple of minutes, the shopping district that I recognized from my explorations around town.

The German couple was speaking quietly with Louisa, most likely asking her to clarify a question, and the Americans were looking ready to get out of the chilly night and find themselves either a drink or a cup of something warm. I'd noticed that the teen boys had hung toward the back of the group ever since Louisa pointed out the mummified cat—did they want a crack at getting in there to take it? But I stuck with them and they never found their opportunity to break away.

"Our final stop on the tour puts us back here at the Angel Hotel, where I know several of you are staying. You might be interested to know a couple of legends associated with the hotel."

She gave them the same information she'd told me

about the tunnel system under the town and the fact that one of the tunnels was known to have originated in the cellars of the Angel. She ended the tale with the story of the fiddler who went into the tunnels to determine where they went, only to disappear forever.

"So, sleep well tonight," she said, "but be sure to let someone know if you hear fiddle music in the quiet hours before dawn."

She dismissed the group, and the Americans from Indiana quickly climbed the front steps of the hotel, no doubt hoping that the hotel bar would still be open. While Louisa conversed easily with the Germans, I noticed that she kept an eye on the teens until a car arrived and a man tapped the horn.

"Your dad, Tim!" she called out to him, giving the man a wave as the boys got into the vehicle.

I took a spot on one of the concrete benches in front of the hotel, hands in pockets for warmth, my mind swirling as I thought about the fact that we would soon be attending Dolly's funeral.

Chapter 16

Monday morning dawned—barely—a day of heavy gray clouds and mist hanging in the air. It seemed fitting for the small gathering at St. Mary's. Although Archie said that Dolly wished to be cremated and have her ashes scattered over the Dover coastline where they had once vacationed, he thought it appropriate to have a little service at the church and for the vicar to say a few words out in the ancient graveyard. We huddled under our umbrellas and, mercifully, the man really did keep it to a very few words.

The gathering could hardly be called a crowd—Archie, Gabrielle, Louisa and myself plus two other women that I guessed might be customers of the knit shop. Both wore handmade sweaters and scarves. As he had on Friday, Archie stared vacantly through the mist, a hollow-looking man.

When Gabrielle extended an open invitation to come by

the shop for coffee and cake everyone accepted in sympathy for the widower. Rumor was that Archie planned to close the shop as soon as possible and that he would soon be moving out of the apartment. I wondered if the two shop patrons were simply eager to see if there might be bargain prices offered on the yarns.

For myself, I had two motives for stopping by. One was to learn the official cause of death. The coincidence between all the events that had so badly upset Dolly, and her death just hours after the last one . . . well, I couldn't let that go without at least asking. My other motive was simply to get out of the rain.

Gabrielle assumed the role of hostess. The table holding the partially burned candles had been cleared and converted to a spot for a variety of bakery-made cakes, plus an urn of coffee and a pot of tea. She sliced the cakes and served them up on paper plates. The other women began openly browsing the yarn bins and when Archie let them know they could have anything for half price even Louisa joined in.

I nibbled at a slice of Battenberg cake, described on the wrapper that I spotted nearby as "a chequerboard of moist sponge wrapped in almond flavoured paste." All I knew was that the cute little pink and yellow squares tasted delicious. I debated sneaking another one but I saw my chance to speak to Archie, who was standing alone near the sales counter at the moment. I expressed my condolences once again, then posed my real question about the cause of Dolly's death.

"The coroner's inquest ruled that it was an overdose of her sleeping medication," he said. He looked stricken. "I just can't believe she would do it."

"Did she often—?"

"Take a sleep aid?" he jumped in, knowing where I was

going with this. "Often enough. My wife sometimes had trouble sleeping." His face seemed to go slack. "If only I'd watched more carefully."

Dolly had once told me she was a light sleeper.

I opened my mouth to ask whether the coroner thought it was a suicide, but Archie turned away and greeted one of the women who'd walked over with her arms full of yarn balls.

There really wasn't a delicate way to quiz the new widower about his wife's drug habits so I backed away. All right, I'll admit that I backed right over to the cake again and took another slice of that Battenberg, asking Gabrielle where she'd bought it while I watched Louisa and her cronies plundering the yarns.

By the time my aunt had paid for a rather large bag of new needlework projects I'd exhausted any possible conversation with Gabrielle and I'd found the spot where they'd stacked the damaged candles and marked them at eighty-percent off. I mentally ran through the list of things that had happened to upset Dolly—the hot and cold tea, the mysterious muddy footprints in the shop, the mixed up coins in her register and scrambled yarns on display. Those things seemed real and tangible and yet we'd found no cause. And then there were the ethereal things—the unexplained noises, shadows and ghostly images, the cold drafts through the store. Although Dolly seemed like a pretty indomitable force, maybe she'd simply reached her limit.

Out on the street, the rain had stopped and the clouds seemed to be thinning. We walked toward Louisa's home, avoiding the larger puddles, and I told her what I'd learned from Archie—that Dolly had died from her own sleeping medication.

"I couldn't bring myself to ask Archie any more detailed questions. Such as, I wonder if the police would investigate this as a suicide."

"An inquest would be a matter of public record," Louisa said.

"Mind if we duck in and ask?"

She helped talk our way into the coroner's office where I asked to see a copy of the record on Dolly's death. A straight-spined doctor in a stiff white lab coat handed me the death certificate. It pretty much said just what Archie had told me.

"Is there any way to tell if she accidentally took this much or if it might have been a suicide?" I asked the doctor who'd handed me the report.

"No way to know ma'am. There was no note, no other obvious signs of suicidal thoughts. Her husband said she'd suffered several upsets in recent weeks but everything was just fine that night when they went to bed."

Fine, as in throwing a fit because her entire stock of candles was ruined.

But I didn't say it.

"So, the police aren't looking at this as a crime?" I wasn't really sure how else to phrase the question. She wasn't attacked by a ghost? She wasn't snuffed out by a phantom presence in the room?

"No, ma'am. You'll notice that it's been called an accidental death."

And that was that.

We left the office, and started toward Louisa's house.

"That's complete poppycock," she said.

"What? Why do you think so?"

"I might not have known her a long time but I knew Dolly well enough to know that she didn't kill herself. And she certainly didn't take that many pills accidentally. One time we were the only two who showed up for knitting group, so we talked about things a little more personal. She had a sister who died of an accidental overdose when she was just in her twenties. Dolly never got over it. Said she was very careful about every medication she ever took."

"Archie indicated that she took them pretty regularly. Maybe she'd taken a dose while they were watching TV, then there was the incident with the candles and she was so upset that she either forgot she'd already taken them or she figured she'd never get to sleep unless she took more."

Her eyes flashed. "This is one thing I know. Charlie, I'm sure of it."

"But the inquest—"

"I'm just saying. Something got those pills into Dolly, but she didn't do it herself."

"I don't know . . . She was pretty rattled over the things that happened to her in the store . . ."

"Can you look into it, Charlie? Please? Just ask around and see if anyone knows anything? She didn't have many friends. I just feel—" Her voice cracked.

That much was true. The pitiful turnout at the service, the number of complaints on record at the police department. Was this a case of a disagreeable person's karma catching up with her, or was there truly a more sinister set of events that had turned against Dolly Jones?

Chapter 17

We grabbed a quick bite for dinner, then snuggled in for the night with the gas fire lit against the bone-chilling damp. Louisa found a comedy on the television but I couldn't concentrate, even with the canned laughter interrupting every few seconds. I spent a restless night, still torn by the pull of going home.

The next morning at breakfast I brought up the subject with Louisa.

"Don't go, Charlie. You're the only one who can possibly find out what really happened to Dolly. The authorities have closed the file. Archie is a mess—poor man can't even think straight."

"You don't actually believe that some supernatural presence killed her, do you?"

She rearranged the toast on her plate. "Well, of course,

not in so many words. But Dolly was a strong woman. I can't see that she would kill herself because she became frightened."

I had to agree with that. Although I'd seen Dolly pretty shaken up, she always came back by either brushing off the scare or charging through in spite of it.

"She would have simply moved her shop when the disturbances became too much bother," Louisa said, "or she'd have seen her doctor if she didn't feel well."

Probably true on both counts. Either the coroner was correct or there was only one other possibility. Someone had killed her.

The police would normally look at the family members. I'd watched enough investigations up close to know that. So if there were any reason to suspect Archie, they would surely be questioning the heck out of him. Plus, just looking at the man yesterday—he was genuinely in shock.

So, who else might have it in for Dolly?

Well, let's see . . . At least a dozen complaints had been lodged against her. Among that group, someone must have taken his or her problem much more seriously than the police did. I supposed I could ask a few more questions, just see where it might lead.

Louisa sat across the table from me, sending a hopeful gaze my direction.

"Okay, I'll stay. I can ask some questions."

"Bethany is back at work and I've taken the rest of the week off. I'll help you," she said with a delighted smile.

There wasn't much way of dissuading her as she bustled around the house, gathering some notebooks and pens, a flashlight, a magnifying glass and an antique walking stick with a dagger-like concealed tip.

"No idea what we need," she said, "so I'm bringing it all."

"I think just the paper and pens will handle it," I told her. I really didn't want to mention that I carry a pistol at home, or that more than a few of my investigations have put me face to face with killers. I had no intention of letting this case go that far. We would ask a few questions. If we found any real evidence at all . . . I would immediately bring the authorities into it.

While Louisa dressed I jotted down the few names I remembered from the police blotter. We should probably go back there first and obtain a complete listing of all the complaints. When she came downstairs—in tweeds and sturdy walking shoes—I suppressed a smile and gave her a short briefing.

"We'll get the names and addresses," I said. "There are quite a few so we should divide the list. Just engage each person in conversation. Do *not* represent yourself as working for the police." I could see us getting into big trouble that way. "Find out if they had seen Dolly recently, and when. If it was within, say, the last month or so before she died ask about the circumstances of the encounter. Was there any problem, that sort of thing."

"Got it."

"If you run across anyone at all who was extremely angry with her, just back away. We'll give their name to the police. I don't want to end up in an English jail for our efforts."

"Right," she said as we walked out the door. "At least it couldn't be nearly as awful as the one in Marrakech."

I stared at the back of her tweed jacket as she locked the front door. Marrakech? Seriously?

She chatted about how lucky we were that the weather had warmed up again, while I thought about all the family surprises I had in store for Ron when I got home.

We got a printout of the complaints from the same clerk, Smith, who'd been behind the desk on my first visit. It was printed in sequence with the more recent complaints at the top of the list. Out on the sidewalk, I strategically tore the page and handed my aunt the half with the oldest of the reports. Surely she wouldn't encounter anyone with fresh anger among those names. I'm used to trouble following me, but my place in family history would definitely have a black mark next to it if I let her get into serious danger during my visit. I was learning that she had a knack for that, all on her own.

We took our lists, notebooks and, in my case, a map of the town and split up outside the courthouse. It was nine o'clock and we agreed to meet at the Angel Hotel for lunch at twelve and compare notes.

I watched Louisa head up the block with a jaunty step before I gave serious attention to my list. Some of the street addresses were vaguely familiar to me after days of walking this part of town. I spotted a coffee house with tables outside and took a few minutes to sit down and fortify myself while I made a few marks on my handy little map. Some of the streets were nowhere to be found, so I assumed they were on the outskirts of town or somewhere in the outlying countryside. For now, I would find the most obvious ones, which were mainly businesses.

The Banyan Tree was a ladies clothing boutique that favored styles with a tropical and Eastern flair. I stuck my notes into my purse and went inside. Sally Darcy introduced herself as the owner and I noted a young woman of Asian descent with dark hair stylishly cut. I flipped through a rack of bright print blouses.

"A lady recommended this shop," I said when she asked if there were anything she could help me to find. "Dolly Jones. She has the knit shop."

Sally's face did a series of little moves, ending with a smile.

"You remember her? I gathered that she shopped here quite a lot." I continued to scoot hangers along the rail, keeping one eye on Sally as I did so.

"Dolly used to shop here." She was sizing me up every bit as much. "Is she a good friend of yours?"

Establish some common ground with your subject. "Oh no, not really. I've only met her a few times. She seemed fairly hard to please."

"If you work in a shop, you'll soon see that side of her." The polite veneer was slipping.

"Oh, I know. Once I heard her get into a terrible argument with a clerk."

"Nearly every time," Sally said. "She did it all over town, but I finally had to invite her not to shop here anymore. Could not please the woman. Well, you see our style here. It's not the sort of thing traditional English women of her age usually buy. But she would spot something pretty and buy it without trying it on. Then she would return it, inevitably. The last time she tried to return something she'd obviously worn and washed. I wouldn't take it back. She threw the dress at my shop helper and kept yelling in the poor girl's face. I had to pick up the phone and call the police before she would leave. She walked out the door saying she would never shop here again."

"I'll bet your poor employee was really upset."

Sally chuckled. "She let loose with some choice words as Dolly left the shop, but she got over it very quickly. We joked that we were glad to see the last of her."

"Did she ever come back?"

"No, and good riddance. I don't need customers like that."

Two women that I guessed to be in their twenties came in just then and Sally put her sales face back on. While she showed them toward a rack of new jackets I murmured a polite 'thank you' and left.

Obviously, Sally Darcy was no fan of Dolly's but she certainly didn't seem the type who would stalk the woman and make her life miserable, much less follow through and slip her a lethal dose of something. I scratched through her name on the printout.

Since the friend-recommended-your-shop ploy had worked so well with Sally at The Banyan Tree, I tried it on a few other stores even though their names weren't on the list. At the bookstore the face of the young clerk went blank at my question and even though I wandered into a different department in hopes of finding a manager, that person didn't seem to recognize Dolly's name either. In a small housewares shop I got a completely different reaction.

"I'm frankly not at all sad that she's dead."

The store owner was a woman in her fifties, who had greeted me with a warm smile and offered complimentary coffee and cookies when I walked in. As with Sally Darcy, Amanda Tremain quickly checked me out to be sure I wasn't a close friend of Dolly's before succumbing to the temptation to speak freely.

"I'd say that she was thoroughly disagreeable," Amanda said, "but that's not how she presented herself. She'd come

across all sticky-sweet at first, do you a few nice turns . . .
liked to curry favor with anybody important. Oh, my, she
catered to the mayor's wife, loved to tell how she'd been to a
party at their home. While her husband was manager at the
sugar factory, she flaunted that around town a lot. It's one
of the bigger employers, you know."

I sipped slowly at my coffee, nodding at her comments,
giving her time and encouragement to tell all.

"You didn't want to let her do you a favor though."
Amanda's eyes narrowed. "You just never knew when you'd
get the knife in the back. I got tired of having her come
here to shop, then criticize the merchandise. Practically
ruined my business, she did. Telling people my products
were inferior, gossiping about me, saying I'd snubbed her
because I wouldn't give her a big discount on account of us
being such dear friends and all. I had my fill of her."

"How recently did she cause all this trouble?"

"Oh, it went on until about a year ago. Once Archie lost
that job of his Dolly had to come down a peg. Tried to make
out that it was her life's dream to have that knit shop, but
I know they moved there to make ends meet. Thought she
had so many friends in this town, she did, and that everyone
would come running to buy from her. Not that one—she'd
burned too many bridges."

I decided to take a chance. "Do you know of anyone
who would have been mad enough to harm her?"

"Is that what they're saying? That somebody killed
her?"

Uh-oh. Amanda could be just as big a gossip as Dolly
and this story might be making the rounds of the town
before noon.

"No, not at all," I hastened to say. How to soften this? "I'd heard that there were some odd incidents at her shop, pranks that left her shaken up. No, the coroner definitely isn't saying anyone killed her."

Amanda looked as if the news disappointed her, but I got no sense that she had personally done anything to Dolly. She, like the other business owners in town, just seemed happy to have her out of their lives. Before Amanda could get wound up with more stories, I changed the subject, ended up buying a small coffee press, and said goodbye.

I still had thirty minutes before I needed to meet Louisa. A utility truck at the curb caught my attention, and I checked my list. Sure enough, it belonged to Raintree Plumbing. I approached the man who was in the process of pulling some lengths of pipe from the cargo area.

"Joshua Raintree?" I asked

"That's me." He set the pipe down and hitched up his pants.

"I understand that you had a complaint against Dolly Jones for nonpayment of a bill?"

"It's about time," he said. "I filed that complaint at the police station weeks ago. Thought you would never get around to investigating it."

He wiped his hands on a rag in the back of the truck, obviously hoping I'd brought the payment to him.

"Oh, sorry, I'm not with the police department."

He studied my face for a moment. "Well, if you're with the court and need information about it, I can tell you exactly what happened."

I pulled out my notepad and kept my mouth shut.

"The lady—Mrs. Jones—called me. Said there was a

leak in the cellar of her shop. Stone flooring was all wet. How much would I charge, she wanted to know. I told her my hourly rates and said I'd come by the place and take a look. Then I write her out a bid after I see the damage. It weren't cheap—had to get special tools to lift that heavy square of stone flooring—but my price was reasonable. And she agreed to it." He punctuated that last statement with a jabbing index finger. "I do the work, *then* she says it's too high and refuses to pay. In fact, refused to pay the whole bill, not only the part she said was too much."

Funny that Dolly hadn't mentioned any of this. She made it sound like Archie handled the whole thing. "So what did you do?"

"What choice did I have? I'd lifted the access cover way under the dirt, crawled in there, fixed a section of pipe, put it all back. Well, except for the stone floor section. Told her the dirt should have some time to dry out first. I told her I'd come back and put the stone back when she had my money ready. And not before."

I made notes, for the sake of appearances.

"You know what I think?" he said. "I think she just got pissed because I tracked mud across that shiny wood floor in the shop. With me boots." He lifted a foot to show me that he wore treaded work boots. "Not like I could help it. Working down there in the mud, you know."

Had Dolly built that incident into something far more? Twisted the story of the tracks on the shop floor to somehow implicate this man?

"So, what'll happen now?" he asked. "About my money."

"I'll present my findings to, uh, the right people and we'll do our best to get you a check." Somehow, some way

I would talk Archie Jones into covering this. It was only right.

Joshua nodded and turned back to the lengths of pipe and I walked slowly on. How could Dolly be so vindictive toward a guy who'd shown up to fix a water leak for her? And then to claim that some unknown entity had made the tracks on the floor . . . maybe the woman really did have a screw loose.

With a glance at the thickening clouds, I pulled my jacket a little closer and quickened my pace toward the Angel. Louisa came in just minutes behind me and we took a corner table where an impossibly-thin girl in black greeted us and took our orders for glasses of water.

"This is harder than I thought it would be," Louisa said, shrugging out of her bulky tweed coat. "Certainly doesn't take them this long to narrow down the suspects when it's on the telly."

I laughed. "No, it's nothing like that, is it?"

We placed our orders for sandwiches. The place was filling up quickly and the cacophony of voices ricocheted off the hardwood floors, mirrored walls, and wood chairs and tables. Fairly confident we wouldn't be overheard, I asked Louisa if she'd learned anything of interest this morning.

"Not a single thing," she said. "Some of the people on my list just said 'Dolly who?' when I mentioned her name. It's no wonder the police don't pursue these types of complaints. A few weeks go by and no one really cares."

I felt badly that I'd given her the oldest parts of the list. But not that badly—my own inquiries hadn't exactly brought forth any hot suspects either. When our food arrived we put our lists aside.

"I've got four more names," Louisa told me as we stood

outside on the steps after lunch. "I'll give them a go and see what happens."

"So I'll see you back at the house when we finish, whatever time that might be?"

She gave my arm a squeeze, her energy revitalized after lunch. I saw a patch of sun on the parking lot and noticed that the clouds were breaking up. The sunshine bolstered my own mood and I consulted my portion of the printout.

The next name on my list was the restaurant owner who'd had a run-in with Dolly over a dog. Funny, I'd never seen a dog at the knit shop or apartment and it never occurred to me that Dolly owned one. I found James Gilcrist at The Bowl and Platter, a vegetarian pub, directing his wait staff in the cleanup after the lunch crowd had left. He seemed like a precise little penguin of a man with a fringe of brown hair surrounding a bald dome, dressed in black slacks, white shirt and black vest.

"Oh, I remember the instance *very* well," he said, with a raised eyebrow.

Chapter 18

Gilcrist lowered his voice and stepped out of the path of the bustling waiters.

"It involved a dog?" I asked. I'd led him to believe I was following up on his police complaint, without actually saying that I represented the department.

"Don't get me wrong. We all love our pets. I can't allow them inside the restaurant, of course, but at the outdoor tables if the dog is kept on leash and minds its manners, that's fine."

"But Mrs. Jones's pet didn't quite do that?"

He rolled his eyes. "First, she wanted to bring the animal inside. One of those little fluffy things, very small. Well, I could envision hair everywhere. I told her it would have to be outside. But it was a rainy day and she didn't want to sit out there. Got very indignant with me, informing me that *this* was the mayor's wife's dog and that it had the *highest* of pedigrees. The mayor himself would be very upset, she said, if he learned how rudely my establishment had treated his wife's very dear friend."

His face grew livid as he went on. "*Then* she set the dog down on the floor and it proceeded to lift its leg on the podium. I stood right there and watched it. The woman didn't even have the good grace to be embarrassed. She merely ordered one of my servers to wipe it up. She proceeded to take a seat at a table and call the creature up onto her lap where he began licking at the salt shaker. I had to call the police before she would leave. It was humiliating—but apparently not for her. She caused an even greater scene by shouting at me as she made her exit. I could have wrung her neck."

"Really?" Maybe this was my suspect.

"Well, you know. It took all afternoon for my pulse to settle to a normal level. My god, the woman truly believed she walked on water." He tugged downward at his short vest, straightening it.

"Did you ever mention the incident to the dog's owner? Undoubtedly the mayor's wife would have heard about this. I'm curious how she took the news."

He drew himself up taller. "I never said a thing. However, I've heard things . . . she did somehow get the word and I heard that she was furious with Mrs. Jones afterward. Two of my customers were speaking of it one day, how Dolly Jones would never be invited to another society luncheon in *this* town." He seemed to have forgotten that I might be making note of his comments, but I didn't want to stop his gossipy train of thought.

With Dolly's love of being connected, this would have

been a serious blow to her esteem. Maybe she'd had words with someone important and things had gone a bit too far. I thanked Gilcrist for the information and left.

So far, my inquiries relating to the police reports weren't netting me any solid suspects. But the more I thought about it, the more sensible that seemed. A person would have to be pretty dim to call in a complaint against Dolly and then proceed to torment her to death. It was far more likely that whoever was behind the pranks would have stayed very quiet about it. Shop owners and businessmen would simply brush her off. This was personal.

Louisa might be able to tell me who Dolly's friends were—if she actually had any. I headed toward her house, ready to settle in for tea or drinks or something, but I passed Lilac Lane and decided to stop in and say hello to Archie.

"I'm doing all right," he said when I asked. That thousand-yard stare was gone, although his face remained long and grayish.

"I see you are packing up the shop." A lot of the merchandise was gone—only some of the bottled oils, a few candles, and the less-desirable colors of yarns remained. Gabrielle stood in the far corner, wrapping each small bottle in paper and placing them into a carton.

"I'll move back to the house near Fornham. I've given the tenant notice."

I'd been under the impression that they needed the rental income and that the apartment in town was much less expensive than their large home, but I supposed with the shop closed there was no real reason he would want to be there. Plus, the apartment must hold painful memories of Dolly's death.

I remembered that I'd made a semi-promise to Joshua

Raintree so I mentioned the plumbing bill to Archie. He obviously had not been told about the altercation but he pulled open a file drawer and came up with the invoice.

"Sure, I'll take care of it," he said, placing it near the cash register.

"Louisa was hoping to stay in touch with the ladies from the knitting group," I said, the lie slipping out before I could catch it. "Would you happen to have a list of them? So she could get their phone numbers?"

He gave me a blank look, but Gabrielle bustled over to the counter. She sent her pretty smile my way. After a minute of rummaging through some loose scraps of paper near the register, she came up with one.

"There you go," she said, handing me a pale green sheet of notepaper. "Don't suppose we'll be needing it anymore."

I thanked her and told Archie to let us know if he needed any help. I couldn't fathom what that might entail, other than moving all that heavy furniture up from the cellar and I instantly began to regret the offer. I scooted out of there before he could think of it.

Down the block I unfolded the page Gabrielle had handed me. There were about a dozen names on it with phone numbers beside them, each in different handwriting, the kind of list people pass around at a meeting to take attendance. Some only gave first names, but Louisa could probably fill me in.

When I reached the house I discovered she'd arrived before me and was in the process of uncorking a wine bottle.

"I'd no idea how exhausting this is, asking questions of people," she said. She'd shed the tweeds in favor of a soft track suit and fuzzy slippers. "Is this what you do all the time at home?"

"And then some," I said with a laugh. All the accounting duties for our small business, the occasional investigation that I personally get wrapped up in, plus keeping up my piloting skills so I can help Drake with his business as well. The thought of Drake made me realize this might be the right time of day to catch him before he started work. I asked if it would be all right to use the phone upstairs.

Unfortunately, I'd forgotten about the additional two hour time difference so I woke him at an ungodly hour in Alaska. He must have been in the middle of a vivid dream that involved me and something lacy because he didn't seem to mind talking—a lot. I closed my bedroom door and somehow twenty minutes went by pretty quickly. When we said a breathless goodbye, I realized that my face was a bit flushed. I ducked into the bathroom and splashed some cold water on it before I rejoined Louisa in the kitchen.

"So—" I said with a too-bright smile as I sat across the table from her. "Did you learn anything from your interviews?"

She gave me a knowing glance and pushed a full wine glass toward me. "Nothing of substance." Her smile drooped a little. "Like I said at lunch, a lot of the people hardly remember what happened. I guess Dolly wasn't nearly as important as she wanted to think."

She made this last comment with just enough hint of humor that I knew she hadn't taken Dolly all that seriously either.

"Well, someone spent a lot of time coming up with those pranks at the shop," I said. "There had to be a reason for that. Someone wanted to harm her and that takes a fair amount of pent-up anger."

She nodded thoughtfully and reached for a bowl of little crunchy snacks that she'd come up with from somewhere.

"Oh, hey," I said, "I've got another list of names we can check."

Her face did a couple of little moves that let me know doing more interviews wasn't going to be tops on her list. I pulled the note page from my pocket.

"I'll do the actual interviews—that's no problem," I said. "But I could use your help with names and background info. They're the members of Dolly's knitting group."

I handed her the sheet.

Her forehead wrinkled a little. "I've never seen a lot of these women at the meetings. Well, guess I can't really call them meetings—we just got together and worked on our projects. Dolly would offer help if someone was having trouble with a pattern or something."

"Do you know them?"

"Most. Some have only given first names but I think I can piece it together." She picked up a pen and began to fill in the blanks.

"Tell me a little about each one," I said when she handed the sheet back to me. I made notes as she glanced at the names again.

"Well, I introduced you to Hazel Blaine at the tourism office," she said. "We work together there, discovered we both love needlework, and she introduced me to Dolly and the shop."

"Does Hazel still, or *did* she still, go to the group?"

"She cut back, said she couldn't spare so many evenings away from home. Has a young child."

"But she didn't quit in anger with Dolly or anything like that?"

"Oh, I don't think so. Hazel is so polite. She might not say anything, even if that were the real reason."

"See if you can find out." It was a stretch—a huge stretch—I knew. Someone polite enough to make up an excuse for not attending would almost certainly not be vindictive enough to go back and torment the hostess. I put a small X beside Hazel's name.

Three other names were of women Louisa knew fairly well and none of them seemed likely candidates either. Again, the tiny X's. If I couldn't come up with absolutely any other clues I might contact them but they weren't on my A list.

By seven o'clock we were getting very hungry and a little tipsy so I suggested that we just pop out to the nearest pub and get something quick to eat. While Louisa changed her shoes I reviewed the list and found that I had four people to definitely contact—the ones Louisa didn't know at all—and four others with 'maybe' beside their names, women she only knew slightly. The calls could certainly wait until tomorrow.

We placed orders at the bar and walked into the larger of the two rooms, looking for an empty table. There, at the first table on the right, sat Archie Jones and Gabrielle. She was feeding him something and smiling widely. Archie spotted me, quickly swallowed and scooted his chair a few inches farther away from hers.

"Hello there," I said.

Gabrielle looked up at me. "Oh, hello." She giggled and I noticed that a tall beer glass at her place was nearly empty. "You should try the sweet potato chips. Yummy, aren't they, Archie?"

"We were just getting a bite to eat after working on the

stock all day," he said, clearing his throat.

"How is it going?" Louisa asked.

"Pretty well. We've sold a lot of the inventory and bagged up quite a lot of trash. I've got a mover coming Thursday for our personal things, the furniture and such. It's just very difficult." He draped his napkin over his nearly-empty plate.

Maybe they *were* merely having some dinner and Gabrielle had a little too much beer.

"Well, I need to be off," he said. He turned to Gabrielle. "You've got your car?"

She nodded a little stiffly and I wondered whether she should be driving, but he didn't seem concerned about it.

"I'll come in again tomorrow then?" she asked.

He gave a quick nod to each of us and made his way out the door. Gabrielle watched him go as she stuffed a few more of the potatoes into her mouth. Louisa, meantime, had spotted a table for us and we took it, just as our plates came out of the kitchen.

"That was odd, didn't you think?" I murmured to Louisa. "Archie and Gabrielle were pretty cozy there."

"Surely it's nothing. He just bought her dinner after a day's work." She unwrapped her silverware from the napkin and started poking at her fish with the fork.

"Probably so." They seemed to work in the shop like a father-daughter team. I decided to let it drop. Suddenly I was starving.

* * *

The next morning I started out fresh and early to go

through the list of Dolly's friends, in one final attempt to figure out what had happened to her. At this point Louisa seemed to be the only one who felt terribly concerned about it, and if I couldn't find some answers pretty quickly I was going to have to talk her into accepting the coroner's report.

Before she left for the office, Louisa had looked up the addresses of my targets and had marked them on my little map, which was by this time becoming rather covered in scratchings and notes.

I'd laid the groundwork for my visiting each of the women by phoning to say that Archie had wanted each member of Dolly's group to have some of the wools left in the shop. The women all seemed flattered by the gift, and no one questioned too deeply as to why an unfamiliar American would personally be delivering them. Now I just had to get Archie to give me the leftover yarns. Sheesh—the things I get myself into.

Forty-five minutes later I left his shop with four separate bags containing a hodge-podge of yarn, but Gabrielle had assured me that each contained enough for the recipient to make a nice scarf. That seemed a good enough parting gift from Dolly to get me into each house.

Mary Ellis greeted me at the door with such a bright smile that I couldn't turn down her offer of cinnamon cake and tea, despite the fact that she was barely over four feet tall, at least ninety-eight years old, and could hardly make it across the room, even using her walker. There was no way this woman had sneaked around Dolly's shop, setting up the pranks against her, much less entered the upstairs apartment to administer an overdose. I knew this within the first two minutes I spent with her but I stayed for cake anyway. What can I say—it smelled delicious.

One thing about the elderly—they usually love to talk and Mary was no exception. I had the whole scoop on the knitting group: who was happy in her marriage, who was not, how many had unruly grandchildren, and which ones were not really very good knitters but just came for the company. But it was all in a lighthearted vein.

"I heard that Dolly could be pretty disagreeable at times, that people around town didn't like her much. That surprised me. She always seemed so nice."

"Well, I can tell you—" she began. "That wasn't always the case." She started in on the mayor's dog story.

"What about those in the knitting group?" I asked, trying for information I didn't already have. "Is that why some of the ladies stopped coming?"

"I only know of one who truly could not abide Dolly Jones in any form." She reached for the tea cozy and refilled my cup. "Elizabeth Scott. Pretty girl. You might say that she has *dated* a few men. I say that's her business and I didn't much care. She was always very kind to me. But Dolly, she just had it in for that poor girl. Spread ugly rumors about her. It got so that Elizabeth lost some of her clients—she's an exercise instructor. All because of Dolly's gossip."

Chapter 19

The fitness center was near the post office. I'd passed it several times but never really taken much notice. Although Elizabeth's name was on my list, I'd not been able to reach her by phone so just dropping in seemed like the best way to handle it. I left the yarn in my tote bag. Somehow I didn't think she would believe Dolly was sending a gift.

A receptionist pointed out Elizabeth Scott who was working out with weights in the far corner of the large room, and told me it would be fine to go over there. I stepped gingerly between the unfamiliar machines and scary-looking heavy weights and made my way to the thirty-something blond in aqua-blue spandex who seemed to be bench-pressing about a thousand pounds of round disks.

"Elizabeth?"

"Yes. Do I know you?" She was barely breathing hard as

she lowered the barbells to the rack and sat up.

"I'm looking into the death of Dolly Jones, on behalf of her friends and her husband."

"She had friends?" She dusted some powdery stuff off her hands. "Sorry. What can I do for you?"

"Dolly was the target of a series of pranks at her shop, right before she died. It really affected her, mentally, and may have had something to do with her death."

Elizabeth stretched her arms into some odd contortions designed to loosen up her shoulders. "I don't know anything about any pranks. Dolly was mental to begin with. I met her because I got started on a knitting project and I found myself in a little over my head. The price of taking private lessons was a bit much, so I joined the group for awhile to get some advice on working the pattern. I finished the sweater—didn't much care for how it looked on me, after all that work. Dropped knitting and the group."

"Did you get along all right with Dolly?"

"At first. The woman ran hot and cold. Friendly one minute, would turn on you the next. She spread some ugly gossip about me, I confronted her once."

"Recently?"

"Two or three months ago, I'd say." Her blue eyes narrowed. "Look, I won't deny that I could not abide the woman after what she did. But I've got better things to do than chase around creating little episodes to scare her. If Dolly was running scared it was probably because she had a guilty conscience about how she treated people."

She marched over to a stair-climber machine and stepped up on it. She pressed a couple of buttons and the machine started moving. "Sorry, I've got to finish my warm-up. I have a class in twenty minutes."

Well, Elizabeth Scott didn't seem like a sneaky poisoner who would slip someone extra pills or mess around with cups of tea or shuffling coins in a cash register. I got the sense that if she were in the mood she could simply break your neck. I left the gym pretty quickly.

Watching Elizabeth in her skinny-spandex, lifting those weights, put me in mind of the exercise I should be doing. I popped into a pastry shop and squelched the mood with a cupcake and take-out cup of tea. At a tiny table outside I sat down to finish my cupcake and consult my map.

Louisa had marked the address of Joanna Sands for me, so I brushed the cake crumbs off my jeans and headed that direction. Her home was on a street so similar to Louisa's—a row of stone houses with colored doors which opened directly onto the sidewalk—that I wondered if people ever got mixed up and went to the wrong house. Joanna opened the door within seconds after I pressed the bell. She could have been Dolly's sister—same height and build, nearly the same age, even the same haircut. She wore a pleated skirt and twin set in pastel blue.

"Mrs. Sands? I'm Charlie Parker. I phoned this morning."

"Ah, yes." Her gaze traveled from my head to my sneakers and back. "So Dolly wanted me to have a gift."

I held out the bag of yarn that I hoped would gain me an invitation inside.

She peered into the sack, wadded the whole thing with her hands and threw it to the sidewalk. "She would! She *would* choose this color for me. I absolutely cannot wear orange!"

"I . . . I'm sorry. I'm afraid I randomly chose them."

She took a step back and drew herself up straight. "Sorry.

Not to take it out on you, but Dolly . . . she simply—" Her face crumpled and her voice cracked.

"Joanna? Are you all right?" Maybe the gift was too vivid a reminder of her friend's death.

I reached into my tote and brought out the other two bags of yarn. "You may certainly have your choice."

"It's not that." She waved them away. "I don't want a gift from Dolly. I should have told you that on the phone this morning. I guess curiosity got the better of me." Her eyes grew hard. "She treated me so . . . so badly. All for the one favor, years of feeling like her slave."

"What—what happened?" I glanced up and down the street, a little uncomfortable with the intimacy of the conversation, right here on the street, but there was no one else around.

Joanna noticed. "You might as well come inside. It's a rather long story."

I followed her into a parlor that was remarkably like Louisa's. She waved vaguely in the direction of the sofa and I took a seat. She remained standing and paced as she talked.

"I got into a bind once. My daughter needed an operation, one not fully covered by the National Health Service. I desperately needed the money and had no other resources. Dolly was a friend. I confided my situation."

She looked directly at me. "You didn't ever want to confide anything to Dolly, as I later learned. At any rate, as soon as she knew about my situation, she became so very caring and concerned, so I accepted a loan from her. It was in the days when Archie made tons of money in his position at the sugar factory, so I knew they could spare it."

"What happened?"

"I paid back the money. My Christmas bonus was a nice one that year, so I gave her most of it right away. The rest came a little at a time over the next months, but I did pay it back."

She seemed sincere enough, her earlier anger almost completely receding.

"But then Dolly began calling in the favor in so many ways. First, it was simple things. 'Joanna, since you're coming by would you mind picking up my dry cleaning on the way over?'; 'Joanna, be a dear and get me a sandwich for lunch.' Of course she never felt the need to reimburse me for all these little things. But I felt beholden so I didn't say anything.

"Then the favors grew bigger and bigger. 'Volunteer to help me on a committee.' Except that she would inevitably become too busy and I would take on all the work. One year I practically ran the town Christmas pageant all by myself! I'm not a young woman, as you've noticed."

I started to assure her that she looked as vital as anyone, but she went on.

"It was that way with the jumble sale, the choral program, the church bake sale . . . I literally could go on and on. By then I'd paid back all the money, but Dolly became a force to be reckoned with. Any time I told her I couldn't take on any more, she would almost literally leap down my throat as she reminded me how she'd saved my daughter's life." She'd begun to twist her fingers practically in knots. "I was at the end of my rope, Ms Parker."

"Did you do anything about it?" Was I about to actually get a confession here?

Her face grew hard again. "For starters, I gave up the knitting group. Then I quit going to her shop altogether.

When I stopped answering my telephone she began showing up at the door. If I didn't answer the door, she would peek in at the windows, her face pressed to the glass to see inside. It was driving me insane."

"Did you report to the police that she was stalking you?"

Once more, she crumpled. "No. I didn't have the heart. Ignoring her seemed ungrateful enough, but to take it to the authorities. No, I simply couldn't. I could just imagine how she probably treated poor Archie, and him such a nice man."

She'd paused near the fireplace and I stood.

"I'm sorry to hear how it ended," I said. "So hard to lose a friendship like that."

She apparently thought I was referring to Dolly's death. "Oh, the friendship was long gone before this past week. You can't classify a tormentor as a friend. Keep the yarn—I wouldn't want the reminder."

With that, we had subtly moved toward the door and I found myself outside. The story ran through my mind as I walked the two blocks to Louisa's house. Here was certainly someone with a real reason to be rid of Dolly. Maybe the pressure had simply become too much for Joanna to handle and she'd broken, dishing out little helpings of passive-aggressive paybacks. It wasn't much of a stretch for me to imagine her donning a pair of work boots and grinning as she made muddy tracks across Dolly's clean floors.

This just might be my best suspect—but drugging Dolly? Giving her enough to kill her? I couldn't be sure about that, not yet anyway.

After cake at Mary Ellis's house and that completely indulgent cupcake I'd bought for myself, I needed protein.

I made a hefty roast beef sandwich in Louisa's kitchen and pondered what to do next. I wanted to call Drake and just hear his voice, but midday here was completely the wrong time to call Alaska. He'd said the job was going well and that he might be home within two weeks. I hated the fact that he and I and Freckles were so spread out in different places. I wanted our little family back together again. Soon.

I set my plate in the sink and tried to decide on a course of action. I wasn't going to get back to Albuquerque any sooner by sitting here doing nothing. I at least owed my aunt the effort of following these few leads. If nothing turned up by the end of the week, I would have to call it quits.

The fourth woman whom I'd planned to take a yarn gift to had told me that she worked in a nearby town all day, but I was welcome to leave the gift at her home. Since my true purpose was to question her, I needed to wait until she got home in the evening. So, with a few hours to spare I decided to drop by the yarn shop again. I'd thought of a few questions I could ask Archie, in my attempt to piece everything together.

A blur of pale blue passed me as I reached the front door to The Knit and Purl.

"Joanna?" She must have dashed right over here after I left her house.

"Oh, Charlie. Hello. I was just—well, it seemed only right to pay a condolence visit to Archie."

I nodded mutely.

"Well, many things to accomplish," she said, hurrying away.

Okay. After what she'd told me earlier, I would have thought Dolly's home and shop would be her last choice of places to visit. And if she'd come to pay a social call, it kind of shot my theory about her being the one to slip Dolly the overdose of pills. I grabbed for the knob, only to have the door swing rapidly inward.

"Arch, dear, don't forget, if you need anything just pop over," a woman was saying. I'd never seen her in the shop before, a lady in her fifties with beautiful skin and chin-length blond hair, recently styled. She wore a tailored dress and coat that looked as if she were on her way out to Ascot or someplace equally high-class.

"Oh! Sorry, I didn't see you there," she said to me, her tone as modulated as the queen's.

I stepped back to let her pass, and she went into the dress shop immediately next door.

A glass bottle hit the floor and the scent of geranium filled the air as I entered the shop.

"Bloody hell," Gabrielle cursed. "I'll sweep it up."

Archie stood near the register, leaning a hip on the counter, the telephone receiver in hand, a slightly dreamy look on his face.

Was it just my imagination or were there far too many women calling on Archie Jones these days?

Chapter 20

Archie put the phone down and gave me a quizzical look. I noticed that his shirt had some kind of food stain on the front and his cardigan sweater hung a little off-kilter, as if he'd not looked in the mirror when dressing this morning. The lack of a woman's influence was beginning to show. Maybe that's why they had all begun showing up, to mother him.

"Do you have a spare minute?" I asked.

The half-smile vanished. I gave myself a kick—of course, he had all the minutes in the world, now that his life had been turned upside down. No job, no wife, no reason to put on clean clothes in the morning.

"I'm sorry, Archie. I—"

"It's fine, Charlie. I've got the time." He ushered me toward the stock room.

I pulled out my notepad. "I'm trying to piece together a few details about those incidents that frightened Dolly so badly. I would appreciate anything you can remember about each of them."

He stood very still.

"Louisa studies the paranormal, you know." Technically, the truth. I pushed on with my questions. "For instance, the time that the tea in her cup went from cold to scalding hot. It happened here, in the back room of the shop, correct?"

He nodded.

"Was there anyone else present in the shop at the time?"

"You'll have to ask Gabrielle. I believe she was working that morning."

He was right, of course. I'd come in a few minutes after it happened and but I'd only seen Gabrielle and Dolly at work. He called the younger woman into the room and I asked the question.

She stared at the ceiling for a full minute or two, trying to remember. "I can't be positive," she said, "but that was the day you came in for Louisa's blue heather, wasn't it? I'm fairly certain that the customer right before you was Mrs. Ellis. The order was a yellow cashmere. I tend to remember people sort of more by what they buy than by their names."

I pictured the ninety-something with the walker and I couldn't envision any possibility that she'd tippy-toed into the back room and messed with the teacups without anyone seeing her do it.

"There might have been someone with her," Gabrielle said. "Mrs. Ellis often gets a ride with a friend from the knitting group. But I don't remember which lady it was.

Only Mrs. Ellis bought anything that day."

I made notes. I could go back to Mary Ellis and see if she could tell me who had brought her shopping that day. If I could remember for sure which day it was . . . and if she happened to remember . . . This was already getting complicated.

"What about the other time, when the hot tea turned cold, upstairs in the apartment, and Dolly swore it happened in an instant? Do either of you remember being there, seeing it happen?"

Gabrielle gave a completely blank look. Archie seemed to think he was home at the time but he couldn't call up any details. I had come along later, once again, but I sure didn't remember anyone else being around.

"Okay. What about any of the other incidents? I'm trying to figure out who might have been near enough that they could have set the scene to scare Dolly. The muddy footprints? The yarns all being rearranged? The candles all being lit?"

They both shook their heads slowly and I realized I wasn't coming away with any usable information.

The door bells chimed and Gabrielle hurried back into the shop. I heard female voices.

"Not to rush you, but I have some calls to make," Archie said. "Arrangements for the movers and all that."

Despite his grief he sure seemed to be conducting business efficiently. I couldn't come up with any other viable questions so I left when he started up the stairs.

In the shop, two women were browsing the remaining skeins of yarn. Of the hundreds that had originally stocked the shop, only a few dozen were left. The woman in black turned away from the yarn and faced the bottles of essential oils. I saw that it was Elizabeth Scott.

"What are you doing here?" I blurted out.

She spun around and stared at me.

"Sorry." Belatedly, I realized how rude my tone had been. "I'm just surprised."

She stared around the shop. "I guess I needed to see for myself. She's really gone."

With that, she spun on her heel and sent the small bells crashing into the glass as she whipped open the door. She headed in the direction of the fitness center without a backward glance at the yarn shop.

I looked around. The other customer's eyes were wide. Gabrielle stared at the swaying strands of bells with an enigmatic look on her face. We must have all been thinking how weird Elizabeth's comment was.

A shape passed the front window and the door opened to admit the expensively-dressed woman who had just left a few minutes earlier.

"Mrs. Devon." Gabrielle said somewhat stiffly. "Back already?"

She had shed the coat but her tailored dress was still impeccable and every hair of her blond coif stood perfectly in place. She carried a small white paper sack.

"Just brought a little something for Arch. I'll just pop up to deliver it," she said with a tilt of her head toward the upstairs apartment.

"He's rather busy—" But Gabrielle's words were cut short as the visitor disappeared through the stockroom doorway.

I sent a puzzled look toward Gabrielle but she was too busy staring daggers toward the back of Mrs. Devon to notice. Well, there's more than one way to get information. I walked outside, stepped over to the dress shop next door and went inside.

Two employees were present. A young one was in the process of hanging dresses on a rack. The other—a classy dresser of about thirty-five—was going through some papers at the register. I approached her.

"Excuse me, is Mrs. Devon here?"

"I'm Diana Devon."

I was momentarily baffled. "A blond woman—"

"Oh yes, my sister-in-law, Catherine. She'll be back in a moment. Would you care to wait or shall I leave a message?"

I noticed a small stack of business cards on the counter and picked up one that said, Diana Devon, Proprietress.

I put on my best I'm-new-in-town face. "Is she the same Catherine Devon whose husband owns the Big D ranch in Arizona?"

She laughed politely, as only the English can at a completely stupid question. "No, I'm afraid not. Catherine is a widow. Her husband was one of the owners of the sugar factory here in Bury."

I pretended to be a little embarrassed at the mix up. "Sorry. I thought I'd heard . . . Well, no matter. You have some lovely things in the shop."

She offered to show me the new autumn line but I begged off, saying I was in a hurry today. I'd glimpsed a price tag hanging at the neck of a summer dress, and even at a half-off reduction it was way beyond me.

The sugar mill. So it was quite likely that the Devons had been acquainted with Archie Jones for a long time. Some instinctual thing told me that Archie had *known* Catherine a bit better since her husband's passing. I wondered whether she'd had anything to do with the knit shop occupying its current location. And I wondered if Dolly had any clue. Somehow, I thought there would have been war on the block if she did.

I pondered all this as I meandered along the streets, finding my way back to that ice cream shop and ordering their monster sundae, the Knickerbocker Glory. I ate the whole thing—the fruit, the ice cream, all the sauces and all the whipped cream—even the wafer. No sense trying to cover up the fact. I knew the minute I finished it that I'd spoiled my dinner in a big way and hoped Louisa hadn't planned anything special, because I would have to disappoint her.

I deliberately waited until I'd finished my ice cream before giving serious consideration to the whole Archie Jones/Catherine Devon question. On the one hand I could see how such a thing might happen—someone had a little too much to drink at the office Christmas party one year or something like that . . . On the other hand, Classy Catherine and Archie? I pictured Catherine in the outfit I'd seen her wearing this morning, then Archie in his stained shirt and lopsided cardigan—the image just did not make sense.

I couldn't see her sticking with an affair like that, especially once Archie had lost his prestigious job. With his days pretty well controlled by Dolly the logistics would become very difficult.

Anyway, Charlie, I told myself, you have to have a few more facts before jumping to a conclusion like this one. I waddled out of the ice cream shop, knowing I better walk off some of that dessert. Found myself again in the Abbey Gardens, where the hard rain a couple of days ago had taken a toll on the flowers. They were starting to show a little autumn fading.

I sat on a bench and reviewed my notes but no new insights leaped out at me. Before I could come to any conclusions, I needed to piece together a sequence of events and see whose face showed up as the puzzle pieces began to fit into place. I put my notes away then circled the gardens twice before heading to Louisa's, where I promptly stretched out on the sofa.

By the time Louisa came home from work, I'd roused myself from my somnolent coma. She offered to make sandwiches for both of us for a light supper, but I couldn't manage even that little.

While she ate hers, I posed the idea I'd had earlier. "Help me make a list of each incident at Dolly's shop and let's see if we can put the clues together."

"The first one I remember was when Dolly burned her hand with the hot tea," I said, starting off the list.

"Yes, but she said she'd just finished straightening all the yarns which had been disorganized when she arrived that morning."

"Right." I jotted down the two events. "We can't possibly know who messed up the yarn display since that happened during the night. We have to assume that the perpetrator was alone. So let's start with the hot tea. When we walked in, I seem to remember a couple of other women being there."

I'd not actually met anyone in town at that point, so I was no help with names.

Louisa closed her eyes in a squint. "This helps me to see my visions," she whispered.

I gave her a minute, feeling a sense of anticipation.

"I believe they were Mindy Hart and Elizabeth Scott," she said. "They weren't together. That's the impression I'm getting. Mindy was browsing the yarns and Elizabeth stood near the candles."

"Did either woman seem like she might have been . . . I don't know . . . admiring her own handiwork or plotting something?" Maybe this Mindy person had somehow messed up the yarns and came back to see if she'd left Dolly flustered. "Were either of them near enough to the stockroom door that they might have sneaked in and microwaved the tea to make it boiling hot?"

"Your American-ness is showing. Dolly didn't even keep a microwave in the shop. She always used the kettle and brewed a cup or a whole pot fresh."

Hmm. I had noticed the kettle on other visits, but that particular time I hadn't thought to check to see if it had recently been used. By the time we got there Dolly was already holding ice to her burned hand and bemoaning the fact that she'd broken a good cup.

"Elizabeth Scott always admired Dolly's Spode. She might have done something spiteful, just to watch Dolly cringe, although I doubt she would have deliberately wanted a cup to get broken."

Elizabeth had told me she'd confronted Dolly two or three months ago—no mention of having been in the shop recently. The omission moved her up a notch on my list of suspects.

"What about the first time the muddy footprints appeared?"

"That was before the hot tea incident, too. Remember, Dolly said she'd come downstairs in the morning and the floor was dirty?"

"Ah, yes. I suspected that Archie had come in late and either didn't realize his feet were muddy or didn't 'fess up to it."

Again, she closed her eyes. "Archie normally wears leather shoes with smooth soles. I'm picturing him on that day and I would swear that's what he had on."

"But if the prints were made the night before . . ."

"Quite right."

"I wish there were a way to get into his closet and see if he owns some boots with treads." Even if we could, though, it was doubtful we'd find anything of use. Archie was in the process of packing up to move. And surely by now he'd cleaned the boots anyway.

"I don't think we'll be able to pin down either of those incidents with the muddy footprints, Charlie. Both times the prints appeared at night and had been cleaned up before anyone else saw them. Dolly was like that, wouldn't want a customer walking in to see anything out of place."

"What about the other time with the tea, the time Dolly swore she'd made a fresh hot cup and then it went ice cold? I had walked up to the apartment and I felt the side of the cup. That tea wasn't just lukewarm, it was downright cold."

"And it was only you and Dolly there?" she asked.

"Archie came out of the bedroom. Her scream awakened him from a nap. Otherwise, no one was around."

"But I doubt Dolly locked the apartment door during the day. She would have buzzed in and out several times a day, likely, so anyone in the shop who went into the back room could have climbed the stairs and gone in there."

She was right, of course. At least she wasn't suggesting that a ghost had turned the tea cold. The only reasonable thing I could think of was that someone had poured out the hot tea and replaced the cup with an identical cup of cold tea. And the *only* real purpose I could see in that was to make Dolly believe she was going crazy. And if she truly began to doubt herself, maybe she really did swallow all those pills on purpose.

Chapter 21

My head was beginning to hurt and I was out of ideas to write down so I doodled randomly on the notepad.

"Louisa? Something else came to my attention today," I said. "The woman who owns the clothing shop next to The Knit and Purl, her sister is Catherine Devon. I learned that Catherine's late husband was an owner of the sugar factory. That made him Archie's boss. And now Catherine is buzzing in and out of the knit shop a lot, making solicitous little gestures toward Archie. I only met her today, but she doesn't exactly seem the type to be interested in his sort, does she?"

Her brow wrinkled. "I wouldn't think so. But, you know, the Archie we see today isn't the way he used to be. He was quite tall and handsome in his business suit every day. And something of a charmer."

"I wonder . . . Some kind of love triangle? Might be the real reason he lost his job."

She nodded slowly as the idea began to take hold. "I suppose it's possible."

"Do you think Dolly knew?"

"Dolly? Oh my! I can't imagine that she would sit still for that—especially putting Archie in such close proximity to Catherine—the two shops next door, and all."

I felt my pulse quicken. "But let's say she didn't know until *after* she'd moved her shop there. Maybe she catches Archie tippy-toeing next door now and then at night . . ."

Her mouth pursed. "Well, Catherine doesn't live above the dress shop like they did. She's got a huge manor estate outside town, but still . . . there could have been clues that Dolly picked up on."

"So how am I going to get either of them to admit to an affair?"

Much less acknowledge driving Dolly to kill herself so she would be out of their way. Or . . . worse yet . . . feed her the pills to get her out of the way so they could be together always.

"The coroner didn't find any reason to believe that Dolly didn't merely take the medication herself, did he?" I asked rhetorically. "So now all the sneaky lovers have to do is wait a decent amount of time before pretending to discover an interest in each other. Archie can grieve publicly for awhile, but no one's going to raise an eyebrow when he marries again within a year or so. Most widowers do."

"There's no proof, you know." Dear Louisa, injecting a cold dose of reality.

"But still, Archie allowed me to investigate this. Would he do that if he truly wanted out of the marriage?"

"But you see, that's the beauty of it. It is just what a grieving man *would* do if he were innocent of any wrongdoing."

"So you think he's sharp enough to have figured out that he better play his role convincingly, knowing that I would find no proof and the official findings would stand. That leaves him clear to finish the little charade and move into Catherine's big house after a bit."

"I think Archie Jones is a lot sharper than we are giving him credit for. His career was in managing people, after all." Louisa got up to bring out the last of the cake and heat the tea kettle.

I passed up the dessert but accepted the tea and when we carried our cups to the parlor I brought my notepad with me. Louisa's point about finding proof of a crime was so valid. I could see Archie and Dolly home, just the two of them, like every other couple in the world. She already had prescription sleeping pills; all he had to do was grind up a sufficient number and slip them into her food or beverage to assure that she would go to sleep that night and never wake up.

He would merely wash the dishes, rinse the evidence down the drain . . . even if the pill bottle had been checked for his prints, there were a dozen perfectly reasonable explanations for that. He'd handed his wife that bottle on many occasions. And being cunning enough to set up the scenario to look like she was losing her sanity or becoming depressed was the perfect way to ensure that either an accidental-death or suicide ruling would be likely.

The only way I could see justice done would be to get either Archie or Catherine to confess. Just how I would do that before Saturday, I had no idea.

* * *

I woke from a dream in which I was standing in a courtroom, grilling Catherine Devon—Perry Mason style—until she cracked and told the whole story. But when I opened my eyes the room was dark and I was no closer to a way to prove my theory. I lay there staring toward the ceiling, debating about going to the police, putting the burden of getting the confession on them.

But I knew what would happen. First, they would remind me that there had been an inquest and an official finding. Second, they would point out that I—silly American who probably watches too much television—didn't realize that I was accusing two of the town's prominent citizens of multiple wrongdoing. Third, they would politely show me the door with a typical British thank-you.

No, without some firm piece of actual evidence this would go nowhere.

I looked at the luminous hands of my watch and calculated that it was only six o'clock last night in Alaska. It was worth a try. I dialed Drake's cell phone.

"Hey, hon. What time is it there?" He sounded genuinely glad to hear from me.

"Way early morning," I admitted. "I couldn't sleep."

"How's everything going?"

I gave him the condensed version, admitting frustration at being unable to prove my theory. "If it weren't for Louisa wanting me to stick with it, and the real sense that a murder has occurred, I'd be ready to hang it up and come home."

"Well, I wish you luck," he said.

We chatted a few more minutes but realized I was adding

to my aunt's phone bill. Reluctantly, I let him go. I'm so used to running everything past him when I'm working a case that it was hard to cope with being half a world away.

I hung up the phone, switched out the light and drifted into darkness, only to oversleep in the morning and arise after Louisa had left for the office. I poured a cup from the coffee carafe she'd left half full and pondered what steps I might take.

I needed more information on Catherine and it seemed only logical that such a luminary of local society would have made the news a time or two. So it was back to the newspaper office where I asked for my buddy Billy Williams.

"Oh, Mrs. Devon, sure. Charity events, fundraisers, she helps them all. And of course when Mr. Devon was alive . . . they made a handsome couple."

"Are the society pages saved in a separate archive," I asked, "or do I need to page through every issue?"

"Ah. We've become quite modern here," he said. "There's those microfilm things nowadays. I don't work that machine myself but you're welcome to it."

He called out to a girl who was hurrying by with a stack of newspapers in her arms.

"Issues from these past three years we've got digital on the website," she said as she shifted the papers to her left hip. Clicking a few keys one-handed, she brought up the site. "Searchable. Just there." The mouse pointer wiggled dizzyingly over a white rectangular box.

"Anything older than this, back to 1950, you can search the microfiche. Beyond that, it's in those bound books in the cellar storeroom." She said this last bit to Billy, who looked as if he didn't relish the idea of digging them out for me.

"This would be post-1950," I said, thanking them both.

Williams stayed nearby. I felt him staring over my shoulder a few times, obviously intrigued with the rapidity of the computer search but not wanting to sit at the desk and do it himself.

I entered Catherine Devon's name and got about forty hits within the archive. Clicking the links one at a time was a little time consuming but I had all morning. Had until my plane left, for that matter.

I backtracked through the past year, saw a short announcement about the opening of The Knit and Purl in the Trahorn Building. A few months before that, there had been a big champagne gala to celebrate the expansion of the sugar mill. A posed photo showed Charles Devon and his management team. Archie in a tuxedo beamed at the camera. Louisa was right—he did clean up well. The caption named him as head of the sales division and the article said the expansion was thanks to the fact that the company had landed a huge order. The two-page spread included a lot of photos. I began to pick out Archie, Catherine, and Charles in several of them. Archie stood speaking earnestly to another man, named Nigel Trahorn, in one candid shot.

Trahorn—as in the Trahorn Building?

I asked, and Billy confirmed it. "I believe it was this one's great-great-grandfather who built it. Could be one generation farther back, though." He seemed to be embarrassed that he couldn't pinpoint it any closer than that.

"No problem," I said. "Your memory is amazing."

My eyes went back to the article.

So the Devons had Archie and his sales division to thank

for a big financial coup. And yet Devon had fired Archie only a few weeks later. It seemed to give more credence to my theory that he'd found out about an affair. An obituary for Charles Devon informed me that he'd died before the construction on the mill addition was completed.

"Mrs. Devon owns it now, you know," Billy Williams said, setting some dusty old papers on the desk beside mine as an excuse to start up the conversation again.

My expression must have been a little blank.

"The Trahorn Building," he said. "She has it now."

I tried to process what this might mean, but he went on talking.

"Nigel," he said with a gesture at the computer screen, "that one. Got himself into some kind of difficulties—some say gambling. Mr. Devon loaned him the money that kept him out of bankruptcy. Took the building in return. He died and she inherited."

Why was I bothering with the newspaper? This guy knew the players, the official stories *and* the gossip.

I pointed to a photo that had both Archie and Catherine in it. "Was there ever anything between these two?"

He peered closely at the screen. "Some said so."

"Could that have had anything to do with Archie Jones losing his job at the sugar mill?"

His head bobbed. "Some said."

I wished I could schedule a meeting with *some* and get all the info in one place.

"I wonder if Charles Devon knew about it." Although I'd merely been musing at that point, his head bobbed again. Seemed I could just play twenty questions with him and puzzle out the whole thing.

With no way to separate his nods into fact or speculation I turned back to the news archive. But my mind wouldn't settle well enough for reading. What if Archie and Catherine had been a long-term item and had cooked up a plan to get rid of both their spouses?

Chapter 22

Okay, this was getting weird. If Archie Jones and Catherine Devon wanted to be together wouldn't it have been far simpler to just ask for divorces? Unless Catherine was not about to forfeit her lifestyle, the estate, ownership in the sugar mill and more to settle down with an unemployed man whose own wife would not go quietly into the shadows.

In a case like that it might have made perfect sense to first get rid of Charles Devon, wait a discreet amount of time, then get Dolly out of the picture too. I felt my eyes go wider at the very idea.

"Mr. Williams? This obituary on Charles Devon doesn't really say how he died."

"Oh, that bit about how donations should be made to the cancer fund—that's true. Lungs. Man smoked like a chimney and it caught up with him. After the diagnosis, it went quickly."

There went my theory. But it didn't mean that the newly single Mrs. Devon wouldn't pressure Archie to free up his own life. And if Archie didn't have the balls to demand a divorce, maybe Catherine had ramped up the pressure and either convinced him to do away with Dolly or she might have administered the pills herself. I chewed at my lip. This could add a whole new wrinkle.

The type of influence she might exert over Archie puzzled me at first, but then it became crystal clear. If he got rid of Dolly he could have a position at the sugar mill—something prestigious without a lot of hours, like chairman of the board or something. If he didn't do something about his nagging wife, Catherine could see to it that he remained unemployed and stuck with Dolly forever. Interesting concept.

It didn't quite explain who had actually orchestrated the pranks against Dolly—Archie's presence precluded him setting up some of them. But still. I had to give this a little more thought.

I thanked Billy Williams and left the news office. I was running out of time. My flight was early Saturday morning, so Louisa had offered to drive me back to London tomorrow afternoon where we could have a nice dinner, see a show, stay in a hotel. It would give us some quality time to end the visit and keep us from having to get up in the middle of the night to make the two hour drive and catch the daybreak flight.

Now that I had some clear suspects and motives I had very little time to act. And if I didn't come up with some hard proof I was still back at square one in trying to convince the authorities that two leading citizens were murderers.

Proof, proof, proof—the word thrummed in my head with every footstep.

The only possible place the proof might exist would be in Dolly's apartment or shop, so I needed to go back there and see if I could find anything at all before Archie had completely cleared everything out. Way deep in my brain I didn't really believe I would find anything. Surely Archie had dumped anything incriminating right away. But perpetrators don't always make the smartest moves in the heat of the moment. It's why all those dumb-criminal stories exist. It was worth a try.

When I turned onto Lilac Lane I spotted a large truck outside the knit shop. Archie stood on the sidewalk talking to two men, one of whom was making notes on pages attached to a clipboard. Uh-oh. Moving day.

I edged past them and went inside. The shop's inventory was gone. Gabrielle was in the process of tying up a plastic garbage bag. The display bins and shelving had been pushed to one side of the room, a yellow rope around the whole lot with a sheet of paper stapled to it. "Not To Be Moved" was written on the page in bold black marker. The sales room had a hollow feeling.

On the way over, I'd cooked up my story and I tested it now on Gabrielle. "The last time I was in the apartment with Dolly, I left something behind. Would it be all right if I—"

She waved me toward the stockroom and the stairs.

Now if I could just do a quick recon before Archie went up there. Even if he appeared, I would use the same story, although it might be a little harder to bluff my way along with him. For the moment, I knew I didn't have much time so I dashed up the stairs and into the unlocked apartment.

What, specifically, would help make my case? I slipped into the bedroom. Dolly's pill bottles might have helped, but there was no sign of them. It was likely the coroner had taken them. I pulled open the nightstand drawers, in case. No bottles. The drawer on the right side of the bed contained a pair of masculine styled reading glasses, a tube of athlete's foot cream, a cell phone charging cord and an issue of a business magazine.

I hurried to the other side of the bed. Dolly's nightstand seemed no more helpful—hand lotion, a black sleep mask, a tube of lip balm, two hair pins and one of those clip-on reading lights for a book. I tugged the drawer a little farther open. A spiral bound book with a cloth cover rested behind the other items. A journal? I grabbed it up and stuffed it inside my jacket.

The floor of the closet contained ranks of shoes, neatly lined up, his and hers. I scanned through his but there was not one pair with treads like the ones that had made the muddy footprints in the shop. I gave the rest of the closet a quick glance then hurried to the kitchen.

A tiny closet held cleaning supplies and brooms. It might be the logical spot for dirty boots to be tossed, but none were visible. I closed the door softly and glanced around the kitchen. Dolly's rose patterned cups and saucers were stacked in cupboards with glass doors. I counted six saucers and five cups, explained by the fact that she'd broken the one when she burned her hand. As I looked around, I spotted the pieces lying in a tidy pile at one side of the worktop. It must have been too hard for Dolly to simply throw them in the trash and maybe she hoped to have it repaired. Still, nothing unexplainable, nothing I didn't already know.

On the far wall hung a telephone and wired to it, an answering machine. Without a thought, I pressed a button which opened the compartment where a miniature cassette tape kept the messages. I plucked out the tape, dropped it into my pocket and closed the little door on the machine before I could talk myself out of it. Bad girl, Charlie.

Male voices grew louder downstairs, probably Archie and the moving men—they could come up here at any moment.

Back in the living room I scanned the visible surfaces, wishing like hell that I'd thought of doing this search earlier in the week when I might have had more time. A magazine rack beside the sofa held a variety of discards and I picked through them and chose a black-covered calendar book, the kind insurance companies send out. Flipping through, I saw that no one had ever used it—this would be the item I'd left behind, if Archie came walking through the door and caught me here.

Think, Charlie! I stared around the room, heart beating too fast, thoughts not clicking effectively. On the same wall where the door opened to the stairs into the shop, I spotted another door, one with heavy panels and two locks. I twisted the deadbolt knob. As I'd guessed, it opened onto a tiny landing and stairs went straight down to the street. At the bottom there were three small transom windows above the outer door, which had a mail slot in it. This was the door that Dolly said they never used.

But someone *had* used it. At the base of the stairs I spotted a dark clump. I closed the living room door behind me and took the dimly lighted stairs slowly, hoping like crazy that nothing would squeak. The object took shape as I approached. A pair of man's boots. With mud on the soles. I may have just found the ghost's footwear.

I lifted one and looked at the tread pattern. As nearly as I could remember, it looked like a match for the prints I'd seen that morning. The boot could very well be Archie's size. It was about the same as the shoes I'd seen upstairs in the closet. I set it carefully back in place, debating.

Okay, so what did I really have here? Nothing I could turn over to the police. Archie would have a ready explanation. He came home, didn't realize how dirty his boots were until he'd walked partway across the shop. So he sat down and took them off, stashed them here so the wife wouldn't get mad, meant to come back and clean up the mess but something interrupted . . . It was a reasonable scenario, one that would make him look rational and me look like a nut case.

I sat down on the bottom step and pulled out the little journal I'd taken from Dolly's nightstand. The woman appeared to be a very erratic journal keeper. At a glance I could tell that two-thirds of the pages were pristine and new. Starting at the front, the first entry was dated more than five years ago. There were two or three entries in that time-frame—I didn't bother to read them. A few pages on, the dates were two years ago. Thumbing to the end I found ten pages written within the last year, these beginning with Dolly's decision to open the knit shop.

Although her handwriting wasn't easy to decipher I found myself reading passages here and there. At the time she'd decided to open the shop, she'd met a lot of resistance from Archie. One entry said, "I simply had to put my foot down. We are doing this, I told him." An entry dated a few

months later said, "It's started up again. I know it. I'll find
out who she is this time, not let it pass like I did five years
ago."

I turned back to the beginning of the diary. Sure enough,
there were entries expressing Dolly's concern that Archie
might be having an affair. He was out late, he traveled a
lot, he was always in "business meetings." But she didn't
know who the woman might be. She demanded that he stay
home, she planned trips for the two of them, she tried to
orchestrate a social set for them outside of his coworkers.
If only they'd had children, she lamented, then Archie
would be irrevocably bound to her. I scanned the ten or
more pages that went along in this vein, but the journal
didn't yield much in the way of facts, just Dolly's thoughts
on how to keep a rein on her husband.

A large gap in time between entries—things must have
gone smoothly for quite awhile. Maybe Archie had stopped
seeing Catherine—or whomever—for a stretch of time.
Then, two years ago Dolly began another crisis and starting
writing again. When this set of entries continued in the same
vein as the previous, I began to scan. Would the woman just
not let it *go*? She didn't offer up a shred of proof. Only her
inner demons seemed to fuel the thing.

Of course, Archie probably really was having an affair.
From Dolly's notes on the things she said to him and the way
she treated him, who would blame him? I became impatient
and turned to the last entry in the book, dated within the
last month, after the mysterious incidents at the shop had
begun happening. "Archie and his woman are at it again,"
she wrote. "This time they are trying to make me think I'm
going crazy. Well, I'm not and I'll not have this. If I have to

chain him to the store to make him stay home, I'll do it."

What? I paused and re-read that last part. Clearly, Dolly was not meekly accepting the idea that she was losing her mind. And nothing about that entry made her sound suicidal. This was a woman with a firm vision and a nutty plan for keeping her husband in line.

I closed the journal and turned the book over in my hand. Did Archie know this existed? Surely not. I couldn't imagine him reading these entries and not confronting Dolly about it, or not destroying the book after her death. She hadn't gone to any extraordinary lengths to hide it so my guess was that he simply never pried into her things. She either felt confident that he wouldn't find the journal, or she didn't care if he did.

That might be a whole new wrinkle—maybe she halfway hoped he would read the entries and, learning how much she wanted him to remain married to her, would simply give up any other plans. This was one psychologically messed up couple.

Heavy footsteps sounded very nearby and my heart-rate flipped into triple-time. The staircase from the shop to the apartment must be fairly close to the one on which I was sitting at the moment.

In a few seconds someone would be in the apartment, probably the men wanting to pack everything in readiness for the move. I gave a quick look upward at the door to the living room, decided against going back in, opened the door to the street and ducked out.

Chapter 23

The details of the journal, plus the cassette from the telephone answering machine were burning holes in my pockets. I felt like I had vital clues here, I just didn't yet know what they were or how they all fit together. I got two blocks away and then pulled out the tape. It was of the micro variety and I wasn't sure what type of machine would be required to play it—but I knew I didn't have one.

Somewhere in this shopping district I'd seen an electronics store. I wandered nearly eight blocks before I spotted it. A guy who could barely be out of high school sat behind the counter, ear buds plugged in, swaying to a beat that I could hear through his skull. I gave a wide wave of my arms to get his attention.

I showed him the cassette and he looked at it as if it were from another planet. "It's from an answering machine," I said.

"Wow—I thought those were all digital."

"In the olden days," I said with a grin, "they used these." I didn't tell him that I'd come across one in my parents' attic that used small reel-to-reel tapes. That admission would place me in the age of dinosaurs, for sure.

"What I need to know is whether you have any kind of machine that can play this?"

He turned it over in his hands. "Yeah, got it."

I followed him to a display shelf of small tape recorders. Lo and behold, there was actually one, a rather dusty unit. I would buy it if I had to but really, just to listen to what would amount to a very few minutes of messages that probably wouldn't mean anything to me anyway.

"Could I demo this?" I asked.

"Oh, sure." He opened the back of it to be sure the recorder had batteries in it, placed some there, and inserted the small tape. He handed it to me and stood there.

"Privately?"

"Oh, right." He moved over to the sales counter and plugged the earbuds back into his head.

I rewound the tape a short way and hit Play. A man's voice, unfamiliar to me. ". . . another few weeks. These things take time."

Not enough info. I rewound the tape again and it began to play in the middle of a message from someone telling Dolly that the book she'd ordered had come in. I let the tape continue to play. That same male voice came on. "Archie, Nigel Trahorn here. Sorry I don't have the answer you want, about the funds, it will be another few weeks. These things take time."

Nigel Trahorn. I knew that name . . . It took a few seconds to click before I remembered that he was the attorney in the photos at the news office. The man whose family once owned Dolly's building. He'd been photographed talking to Archie at a social function. And now he was calling Archie about some money.

The tape was blank after that. There was no date or time recorded with the message, so I had no way of knowing how recently Trahorn called. I rewound the tape once more. Three messages back, a woman offered condolences on Dolly's death and expressed regrets that she'd not made it to the funeral. That had to have come in after Monday. So all the messages after that were very recent.

So, what money would Archie be discussing with an attorney? An insurance policy, an inheritance, or tax issues were the first things that popped into my mind.

I glanced toward the young clerk who had his back to me, bobbing to his own beat while he ran a dust cloth over merchandise that hung on the wall behind the counter. He may not have even remembered I was in the shop. I might as well learn all I could.

I rewound the micro tape to the beginning and played all the messages this time. They came from the days immediately after Dolly died, which made sense when I thought about it. In her efficient way, she'd probably cleared the tape every time she retrieved messages. Archie merely let them accumulate.

The entire collection consisted of a total of four condolence calls—all from women—then the one about Dolly's bookshop order and the one from the attorney. Clearly, I'd exhausted any possible useful information I would get from it. I ejected the tape, pocketed it, then set the recorder back on the shelf. The clerk gave me a rhythmic nod to the beat of his own music when I stepped over to the door and mouthed a thank-you to him.

Money changes a lot of things, and the realization that Archie was waiting to come into something could be a game-changer. Catherine already had money. I couldn't see that Archie's money would make much difference to her. Although his financial status might. If he could afford to move back to the nicer neighborhood, fit in again with her social set . . . well, that might make it more feasible for the two of them to really become a couple.

On the other hand, why? If they'd continued their affair through the years when Archie lost his job and lived in the apartment above his wife's knitting shop, Catherine couldn't be all that hung up on his finances. I couldn't quite wrap my brain around all the nuances, but then it could just be that I'd skipped breakfast and it was well past lunch time and I needed fuel.

Knowing this would be my last lunch in Bury, I couldn't resist—it was back to the Cornish pasty shop for another of those special treats. I carried the hot little pastry pocket of savory meat with me, picking at bits of the crust while I strolled the streets, mulling over the mountain of little facts I'd gathered about Dolly, Archie, her death and his secret life. Although the details were numerous, I couldn't for the life of me piece together a murder out of it.

In this day and age, people didn't risk a lifelong prison term because they were unhappy with their spouses. Well, okay, some did. But Archie didn't fit the mold. I got it that he had a hard time standing up to Dolly. Her own diary entries made it pretty clear that she was a heck of a determined woman. But the man had two legs—wouldn't he have simply walked out the door if he were ready to end the marriage?

Again, I came back to the money. Depending on what

type of 'funds' Nigel Trahorn had been talking about, and how much it involved, that could very well be the piece of the puzzle that would make everything fall into place.

I wondered how I would find out. Dolly might have had a large life insurance policy, or perhaps there was money in her name that Archie couldn't access unless she died. But even if I had the name of the insurance company or the registration information for a bank account, what were the odds I could bluff my way in and learn the details?

I realized that my little meal had vanished and I was standing near one of the hanging flower baskets at the east end of Lilac Lane. Bluffing is something I do pretty well, so before I could talk myself out of it I strode over to the storefront where a man was in the process of taking down The Knit and Purl's hanging sign.

I sidestepped him and went inside.

"How's it going?" I asked Archie, knowing at a glance that he was in a muddle again.

He was alone in the shop, although I could hear voices of the movers down in the cellar. Archie's hands fluttered above a file box which he'd begun to fill with folders from the drawers of the work area.

"I sent Gabrielle out for some lunch and she's not returned yet," he said.

The phone rang just then, apparently someone who was coming to pick up the store fixtures and wanted to know if this was a convenient time. Archie said it would be best to allow another hour.

"They'll be wanting this counter and the desk," he mumbled.

"Could you use some help? I'm pretty good with paperwork," I said with a nod toward the box.

"I could gather those up, file them neatly. You can always go through them later on, once you get settled."

He lost a little of the deer-in-the-headlights look.

"Here," I told him. "you pack the small items into this box. I'll get the files organized into this other one."

I handed him a mid-sized cube of a carton and gestured toward the clutter of little office items—stapler, tape dispenser and such.

"It doesn't much matter if they're neatly stowed," I said. "Just fill the box and get one of the movers to take it away."

He followed directions well, and I guessed it was from years of practice. Once a woman entered the room Archie Jones just let her take over. A little weird, I thought, but in this case I planned to use it to my advantage.

I pulled the banker's box up beside the two file drawers and took a seat in the chair beside them. Even though I pretended to work quickly, I managed to get a look at each of the descriptive tabs. Everything looked pretty standard for any small business. There were folders for Paid Invoices, Accounting, Customer Contacts and a series labeled with business names that appeared to be the suppliers of various inventory items. I came across one titled Insurance, which I discreetly slipped under the box.

Archie filled the carton I'd handed him and muttering something about needing another one, went off to the stockroom.

I slipped out the insurance folder and opened it, keeping one eye toward the doorway where Archie had gone. Unfortunately, the policy inside was to insure the contents of the shop, not Dolly's life. I filed it and continued.

When Archie didn't immediately appear I took a peek inside another folder labeled Bank Account. It too, was strictly business. The neatly folded statements were all in the name of the shop and the balance on the most recent one showed only about a hundred pounds in the account. Nothing else in either of the two drawers appeared to pertain to funds or money that might reasonably be the subject of the conversation with Archie's attorney.

I quickly jammed the rest of the folders into boxes and placed them against the far wall, well out of the way. When Archie came back I was standing there with a spare banker's box in my hand.

"What about upstairs?" I asked. "I could box up any files you've got up there."

His attention was drawn to a man in work uniform who'd appeared in the doorway.

"We're to disconnect the telephone," the man said.

Archie, clearly no multi-tasker, set down the carton he'd brought for the final office supplies and showed the man where the phone line came in.

I pointed toward the ceiling, a questioning look on my face and he waved me toward the stairs. That was pretty easy. I didn't wait for further instructions.

With permission to enter the apartment and carte blanche on any files I might find up there I scoped out the place. The living room was pretty well filled to capacity with a sofa, two fat armchairs, a TV set and stand, and a coffee table that was way too large for the confined space. Clearly, all their furnishings had been purchased for larger quarters. I didn't remember anything in the kitchen or bath that could remotely contain what I was looking for, and the only other choice was the bedroom.

I'd not paid a lot of attention on my previous visit but now I noticed two good-sized boxes on a top closet shelf. I pulled them down. One was filled to capacity with photographs and personal letters, the family memorabilia that collects in the twenty-plus years that Archie and Dolly must have been together. I ran my hands through the packets of prints without opening them. The envelopes appeared to contain greeting cards, with a few personal letters tossed in. All were handwritten, many on pastel stationery. I turned to the other box.

This was more like it. There were folders with income tax information. The forms were unfamiliar to me but the general gist of declaring one's income to the government and paying a portion of it remains the same just about everywhere, I suppose. The only remarkable thing was that the amount of income on the most recent form, after Archie's forced retirement, was dramatically less. I could see how the couple might have struggled with the change in lifestyle and finances.

Another folder contained two insurance policies. I glanced at the door to be sure no one had sneaked up on me before opening them. The policy on Archie's life had a payout that equaled about three years of his former income. The one on Dolly was for much less, only about ten thousand pounds. It certainly wouldn't make Archie wealthy enough to risk a prison sentence in return.

At the very bottom of the stack, was a large brown envelope. I pulled it out. The printed return address showed that it came from a law firm in London. It had been mailed to Dolly Hempsted Jones. Another quick peek toward the door while I bent the metal brad upward to open it. A document of about twenty pages came out, accompanied by a single-sheet letter on law firm stationery.

Dear Mrs. Jones,

Pursuant to our telephone conversation on this date, enclosed please find your father's trust documents. As per the provisions of the trust, the entirety of Brian Hempsted's estate is hereby placed into an investment account with the firm of Rodgers, Salen and Flagg. Further in accordance with your father's wishes, your inheritance consists of the income generated by said estate, payable to you in an annual sum, for the first five years following his death. Upon the fifth anniversary of his demise, the entire estate passes to you.

Of course it was your father's wish that you leave the bulk of the inheritance invested and adjust your lifestyle to living off the income alone. That, however, is your choice five years from now.

It was signed by the partner named Flagg. I looked at the date on the letterhead. Dolly would have come into her full inheritance three months from now. A chance comment came back to me—she'd told Archie she had the money for something. I didn't know what they were talking about at the time. A brokerage statement included in the packet showed an account balance of well over two million pounds.

You can afford a *lot* of nice little somethings with that kind of cash.

A more important question came to mind.

I turned through the stapled pages of the actual trust document. It was written in typical triplicate-legalese wording but I was looking for one thing. And I found it. Upon the death of the beneficiary, the estate would pass to the beneficiary's legal next of kin, her spouse. If she was unmarried at the time of her death and had no children, the estate would pass to the Royal Society of Orchid Growers.

Here, surely, was Archie's motive.

Chapter 24

Istuffed all the pages back into the brown envelope, pondering.

In the days when he held his management job he probably pulled in about the same income that Dolly got from the interest on her trust. But his losing the job changed the whole picture. Archie could never get divorced from Dolly. That much was clear. And he didn't dare wait until she inherited it all. The Orchid Society might be her father's pet project but I doubted it was Dolly's. She would have pulled the money from her trust as soon as legally possible and she would do anything with the money that she wanted. Including writing Archie out of her will if he did any little thing to piss her off.

Poor, passive Archie. I'd often wondered how a man so dynamic in the workplace, with his winning sales team and all the business perks had become so dominated by his wife. The money was probably the answer.

But even a docile pet will strike out eventually. And perhaps Archie had reached the breaking point. In love with another woman, knowing that in a few months Dolly had the power to cut him off financially, living with the knowledge of the severe penalty for divorcing her. The only solution, it seemed, was to get rid of her.

I stared back at the box of papers. Afternoon sun came through the room's one window, the square of brilliance hitting the brown envelope. I could say that I saw the light but that would be way too corny. I only knew I had to get this information to someone in authority. The sensible, legal thing would be to copy down the name of the law firm in London and put them in touch with the police. But sometimes sensible and legal are a little too iffy and way too slow for me.

Archie wasn't going to look through every item in the house—he was moving, things would be in a mess for awhile. I grabbed the trust documents out of the brown envelope, folded and stuffed them into the inside pocket of my jacket.

The apartment door opened. Yikes!

I pulled some random papers from one of the other files and stuffed them in the envelope as replacements, jammed the packet back where I'd found it and used the roll of packing tape I'd brought with me to seal both boxes shut.

By the time Archie entered the bedroom I'd stacked the two boxes by the wall, making a show of brushing dust from my hands.

"These look like memorabilia so I just taped them up,"

I said. I stared into the open closet. "I was wondering if you had plans for Dolly's clothing or if I should just bag it up for charity."

He gave me a firm stare and I hoped my guilt, or the bulge in my jacket, didn't show.

"Ah. Sure. Charity is fine."

"Do you want to go through the items yourself?" I asked, adding as much sympathy to my tone of voice as I could muster.

"No, it's all right. I wouldn't know what to do with them." He walked over to the nightstand where he'd left his wallet. He gave me one glance, thumbed through the cash, and apparently satisfied that all was intact, started for the door. "Need to reimburse Gabrielle for the lunch she brought me."

I transferred the legal papers and Dolly's journal to my purse and looked around the room for any other evidence of my intrusion.

Although my inclination was to run and run fast, some sense of obligation told me that having promised Archie I would bag up Dolly's clothing I should stick with the job. I found plastic trash bags in the broom closet and hastily emptied drawers of lingerie and sweaters, then pulled the hanging garments from the closet and bagged those as well. I didn't touch the collection of costume jewelry, but I did put the cosmetics and creams from the bathroom into the trash. Duty completed, and having a reasonable amount of work to show for the time I'd spent in the apartment, I went back down to the shop.

The stock room looked like a tornado had passed through. The large worktable in the middle was littered with boxes, mostly empty, and the shelves contained only the ragged remnants of unsold merchandise, things Gabrielle must have taken from the displays and stashed here for lack of anything better to do with them. The tea kettle sat, cold and unplugged, on the short counter where Dolly always kept it along with several utilitarian mugs. She'd apparently learned to leave the good china upstairs.

Voices came up the stairwell from the cellar, the one-word commands of the moving boss and the responding grunts of his helpers. I could hear Archie's voice, nearer, and Gabrielle responded from somewhere farther away down there.

I wandered into the sales room. Outside, the lane was filled with pedestrians, people getting their shopping done before end of day. A normal day in a normal enough setting. The moving van sat at the curb, partially filled.

Catherine Devon passed the window and came inside, wearing a rich bronze-tone dress that set off her blond hair amazingly, with a long coat in geometric print, heavy gold jewelry and pumps that had to be dyed to match. Her smile perked up when she saw me—or was she merely flashing that confident look of a woman who knows she has out-dressed you by miles? I knew my jeans and jacket must be dusty but I refused to look.

Archie walked into the shop, over to the register.

I busied myself restacking the boxes I'd earlier placed at the edge of the room, pretending to make space for more. I'd not seen the two lovers interact all that much so it was interesting to blatantly spy a little bit.

From the cellar below, the workingman voices grew louder as the movers apparently wrestled with those large pieces. Catherine walked straight to Archie and as she spoke quietly to him, I saw her run her long fingers down the sleeve of his plaid shirt. Their eyes met but he quickly averted his, instinctively checking the rest of the room. He spotted me and went back to bagging up the money from the till. Gabrielle came in from the stockroom, made an impatient sound and I saw that she was wrestling with a large garbage bag. She got it tied shut and dragged it toward the door.

"Looks like everything will soon be gone," I said, realizing that Archie had looked up with a what-can-I-do-for-you stare.

He put on his grief face again. Even with what I knew of Dolly's inheritance, I couldn't be sure of his emotional state. I'd seen cases where a spouse who seemingly couldn't stand the other—brink of divorce and all that—suddenly went into deep anguish upon the death of the partner. Belated remorse? Guilt? Maybe that's what was happening here. Of course it was entirely possible that Archie was doing a great job of selling the act. He'd been a salesman for a lot of years.

Catherine had stepped back a little, maintaining a proper distance, but her eyes went often to Archie's face and I realized that she genuinely cared for him. My thoughts vacillated back and forth. Cold blooded killers, or star-crossed lovers?

"Comin' through, please," a burly man's voice called out.

Two men appeared at the stockroom door awkwardly balancing the big leather sofa, the one I'd napped on during that very long night when Louisa and I had stayed here on our ghost hunt. I tucked myself against the wall. Gabrielle was at the door, returning from taking the trash bag somewhere, and she held it open for them using one hand to dampen the sound of the little bells. As the sofa passed through she gave the back of it a stroke with one hand, admiring the soft leather.

"Well, I'd best be off," Catherine said. Her tone was bright but her eyes were on the dust motes floating in the air in the wake of the sofa. I imagined that she didn't want her expensive clothing to get dirty.

She tapped her index finger twice on the counter near Archie's arm, a private little goodbye. There wasn't much point in staying subtle now—the wife was gone and everyone in the room quite easily picked up on the nuances. I returned the pleasant smile she sent my direction as she walked out the door.

"You're about finished, then, Gabrielle?" Archie asked. "Thompson's should be by soon to take the fixtures. That's about all for the shop. I'll need to turn your key back."

The younger woman looked around but it seemed her duties were done. She reached into her jeans pocket and extracted a key ring, from which she worked one key loose. She stepped behind the sales counter and placed it there, then she reached out to give Archie a hug.

"I'll miss you," she said with a glance toward me, "and the shop and the customers, of course."

He patted her back, tried to extricate himself, succumbed to a longer hug. About the time he was going to physically pry her arms off him, she broke away.

"Well, then," he said.

"Stay in touch," she told him. "I'll make you dinner anytime, you know."

I caught the wistfulness in her voice. When he rounded the counter, creating a barrier between them, she didn't have much choice but to leave.

The moving men clumped back into the shop. "It'll require two days, sir," said the senior guy. "That cellar's plumb full, heavy stuff, the stairs."

Archie didn't look happy with the verdict but didn't have much choice about accepting it. The day was getting late. I realized Louisa would probably be off work soon. I made a token gesture to help some more but he wished me goodbye and I headed toward The Nutshell Pub to meet my aunt. We had agreed we should have a drink there on this, my final evening in Bury.

The lights were still on in that electronics store where I'd listened to Archie's message tape and a neon sign in the window said "Copies." Without thinking twice I ducked in and used the self-service machine to copy all the documents I'd taken from the Jones apartment. Depending on my next conversation with Archie, I better be ready to turn these over to the police in the morning.

Stuffing all the pages into my purse I set out once more and came to the tiny pub where I spotted Louisa standing outside.

We squeezed onto one of the two built-in corner benches in the cramped area, which surely couldn't be more than a hundred square feet total, with close to twenty people filling the space and spilling out the open door. Once I got past the mummified cat that hung from the ceiling and the various other heads of dead creatures adorning the walls, the place did hold a certain charm. Louisa caught me eyeing the cat.

"I was just remembering what you told us about the cats being entombed in the walls. I wonder if a mummified cat would only catch mummified mice." I glanced up at the stiff carcass again and found myself casually draping my hand over the top of my wine glass, just in case of drifting skin cells or something.

She chuckled. "The collection in here was once far more extensive. The health department made them clear out a lot of it."

Reassuring.

Two young guys in black T-shirts manned the bar and the crowd was a lively one. With no possible way to have a private conversation, the banter merely bounced around the narrow room and anyone who wanted to could join in. A girl who barely made the legal drinking age flirted outrageously with a slick guy in a leather jacket. He dropped F-bombs liberally as he regaled the crowd with a tale of how he'd managed to elude the police on his motorcycle after a little altercation at an intersection in Stowmarket. Between his exaggerated accent and the hip slang, I probably got only half of that right.

We finished our wine, set the glasses on the bar, and edged through the crowd and out to the sidewalk. The close little neighborhood hid any true view of sunset as I'm accustomed to it in the wide-open spaces of New Mexico; this was more like a gradual dimming of the light.

"I know a charming, very out of the way place where they serve a hearty dinner, if you'd like," Louisa said. "We'll go past St. Mary's, then it's just a short way."

After my investigative afternoon, my head becoming crowded with way too much information followed by the noise inside The Nutshell, the quiet street provided a nice respite. I gave myself over to simply enjoying the historic buildings, the hanging flower baskets under soft street lamps, and the relative silence now that workers were closing up shop and heading home for the night.

Over a nice cut of beef with mashed potatoes and steamed vegetables I told Louisa about my findings, from my visit to the news office to the subtle glances I'd caught between Archie and Catherine.

"I'm afraid to admit that I did a little pilfering too." I held up Dolly's journal and told her about the trust fund. "I keep going back and forth, wondering if Dolly's over-possessiveness is all that's behind her writings and the things that were happening in her shop."

"Or, did she genuinely have something to worry about? With an inheritance of over two million pounds coming to her, maybe she really did have reason to be worried." Louisa sipped at her wine.

"I also have to admit to making copies of the documents. In case the police need the evidence. But they don't even believe there was a crime. I don't know what to think."

Louisa's blue eyes looked sad. "And now you're leaving tomorrow. I wish you could stay longer."

I had the feeling that she'd come to enjoy having someone else around the house, a pal to do things with. I felt a little sadness too.

"Well, I will just have to come back. Or you'll have to come to Albuquerque. The house is certainly big enough to accommodate a guest for awhile."

"Yes, without your father it would—" She gave a tight little smile.

I felt a lump rise in my throat, a type of regret for events past, even though I'd not even been born when it all happened. There seemed to be so much still unsaid. My mouth opened, then shut again.

Louisa drained the last of her wine and put on a bright smile. "Let's don't allow your final evening to be a downer in any way, okay?"

I nodded.

Our server came up behind me and before I quite knew what was happening had delivered the check into Louisa's graspy hand. We did a little haggle over who should pay; I still felt that she had saved me a fortune in hotel costs. But she had her money out and I acquiesced. Treating me to the nice dinner seemed like something she genuinely wanted to do.

"Come on, then. Let's get on home. I've bought another of those Battenberg cakes you loved so much. We'll make a cup of tea."

We walked out into the quiet evening. A lone bird called out somewhere, and in the far distance the sound of traffic drifted over from the A14. But the neighborhood streets were nearly silent now at the dinner hour.

"I have to admit that I'm feeling a bit guilty now about taking Dolly's papers, particularly the journal," I said as we crossed the street. "Even though Archie might not want to know what she wrote in there, the book itself belongs among her things."

"Truly? Even if he might have been behind her death?"

I raised an eyebrow. "Well, I did make those copies."

She chuckled.

"Why don't you go ahead and start the tea," I suggested. "I'll pop over to the shop. Archie will either be upstairs or he'll still be working at packing up. If I don't see him I'll just drop this through the mail slot. That way you and I have all day tomorrow to have fun and make the drive to London."

"It's quicker if you cut along the path beside the church," she said. "If you aren't afraid of the graveyard's residents." Her lopsided grin made the suggestion into a dare.

"Me? I ain't afraid of no ghosts!" I turned right, humming the *Ghostbusters* theme song while she continued to the left and home.

Chapter 25

The path beside the heavy old Gothic church was quiet and deserted. Ahead, a lone streetlamp glowed but it seemed far in the distance. I pulled my blazer tightly against the damp and picked up my stride.

To either side of me drops of dampness hung on the thick grass. The old grave stones were black chunks rising from silvered lawns. That theme song wouldn't leave me alone, even though I made a conscious effort to switch to something less vivid, a classic waltz perhaps. Ahead, mist swirled around that distant streetlamp.

Okay, Charlie, this is just way too movie-set freaky. I tried humming an old Creedence Clearwater tune but the notes came out reedy and the weak sound just bounced off the stone walls around me, making it seem that voices were coming from all sides. I quickened my pace again but refused to break into an all-out run.

Finally, it felt like four hours later, I passed under the street lamp and the cross street was visible on the other side. I knew where I was—one block over and three up, and I would be at the shop.

At the next intersection cars were driving along in perfectly normal fashion and laughter from a pub came out along with a bright square of light that hit the sidewalk. *See, silly, there was nothing to worry about.*

Without the carved wood sign above the door, I didn't immediately spot The Knit and Purl. But then I realized the moving van still sat there, all closed up and dark. The men must have quit for the day but left the truck rather than taking a chance that their prime parking spot would be gone in the morning.

The shop itself was dark except for a light coming from the stock room. A shadow crossed the rectangular doorway. Archie must be working in there. I glanced toward the mail slot in the other door, the one that led up to the apartment.

It would be simple enough to drop the diary and the legal papers through the slot and not have to admit that I'd taken them. But what if Archie were not the one to find them? What if he didn't check there before completely vacating the premises and someone else came across them? They contained information far too sensitive and personal to leave to chance like that.

I tried the door to the shop but it was locked. I tapped at the front window. Twice. Finally, Archie peered from the stock room, a silhouette against the golden light. I pressed my face near the glass so he could see who was there.

"Charlie? What is it?" he said when he opened the shop

door to me. He'd forgotten to remove the dangling string of bells and they tinkled just as happily as in the days when customers came in.

"I need to talk to you," I said.

The store's fixtures were gone, leaving the small room feeling cavernous and hollow. Without the sales counter or display shelves the only signs of the former shop were dustballs and a few random bits of trash. The boxed files and office supplies sat near the door to the stock room.

He ushered me forward. "I've been clearing up the last of the things in there. Once the buyer came and took the fixtures away it seems quite barren in here, doesn't it?"

I followed him to the back room, where it appeared he'd made quite a bit of progress. A few boxes were stacked against the wall and the metal shelving was dismantled now. The large work table in the middle of the room still held a ton of clutter.

He looked oddly relaxed, completely businesslike. I still had a hard time picturing him grinding up pills and putting them in Dolly's food. He seemed like a man quietly going through the motions of adapting to a new life.

"Archie." I cleared my throat and wondered if this was the best approach. "I know about the affair."

He looked up from a box he'd just taped shut, his bland expression giving away nothing.

"You and Catherine Devon. Dolly suspected it for a long time." I held up the journal.

He gave it a cursory glance, as if he'd never seen it before.

"I don't know—"

"You do know what I'm talking about."

"Actually, Ms Parker, I was about to say that I don't

know that I want to discuss this with you."

"Fair enough. You don't owe me an explanation." I set the journal on the work table. "But you did ask me to look into Dolly's death because you didn't think she purposely took those pills."

"And I still don't believe that."

"But don't you see? If the police were to look into it, wouldn't you be the most likely suspect?" I lifted the sheaf of legal pages. "You certainly have the most to gain from your wife's death."

"What've you got there?"

"Archie, surely you've seen this? Dolly's father's trust. He left her quite a lot of money. I tracked it down after hearing Nigel Trahorn's message on your answering machine."

I took the micro tape out of my purse and set it with the journal.

"I'm sorry that I took these things from your apartment, but I was following your instruc—"

I swore I heard the bells at the front door. Archie must not have locked it after I came in. I stepped to the doorway and peeked out, only to find myself face to face with Gabrielle.

Her eyes went wide, matching my own I felt sure.

"You too!" she said.

What? I backed into the storeroom and bumped into the table.

"What are you doing here with him?" Her peach complexion was now suffused with blotches of red, her eyes wild.

"Gabri—"

I have to admit that I barely saw it coming. She advanced on me, picking up one of the steel cross pieces from the metal shelves Archie had disassembled. She grasped the thing like a baseball bat and swung it at me. I stumbled around the work table, backing away from her wild movements. The cellar door stood open and she drove me toward it. My foot went off the edge of the uneven stone landing. I felt myself cartwheeling into space.

Everything went black.

* * *

A hazy roar sounded in my ears, like the steady pounding of surf on a windy day. My eyes tried to open but felt heavy and dysfunctional. One lid raised partially, my vision blurred, it closed again. I gave in to the feeling, succumbing to the desire to sleep.

Voices intruded—one male and one female—but I couldn't make out the words. The roar in my ears kept intruding. Everything felt cold and rough and painful. I rested again but something deep inside warned me not to allow myself the luxury of real slumber. I stretched the fingers of my right hand, felt a hard surface like concrete. It was cold to the touch and I began to realize that my whole body ached with it. I squeezed my eyes tight, trying to work up enough moisture to open them.

When I finally peered out through a web of lashes, all I could see was a nondescript expanse of gray, heavy shadows, large unfamiliar objects. I blinked again and worked to make the other eye open. A ghostly image moved in the distance, but when I got both eyes to focus on it I realized it was a foot in a smooth leather shoe.

". . . ready, my darling," said the female voice.

A mumbled response in deeper tones told me that the

man had replied but I couldn't understand his words. My hearing remained muffled. I wanted to shake myself, like a dog, rid myself of the hurts and the fuzziness.

"Soon," she said. "I shall . . . soon." The words faded in and out but the voice was vaguely familiar. Gabrielle.

Footsteps sounded crisply—tap-tap-tap-tap—across the floor, then a more uneven pace. I tried to turn my head to see where they went, but the tiniest motion sent excruciating pain and a wave of nausea through me.

A thump, somewhere above me. I closed my eyes again.

"Ms Parker?" A small touch on my shoulder woke me. "Ms Parker, wake up. Are you all right?"

Do I look all right? Something inside told me that I must be fine if I could conjure up that thought.

I wiggled my fingers again, brought my right hand up to my face. It came away bloody.

"Ms Parker, it's Archie Jones. Please wake up."

I must have drifted off again for a second there. *Okay, Charlie, you have to get moving.* I rolled over to my back and stretched my legs out. I must have been lying on my left side, fetal position, for quite awhile. The bones felt like they'd flattened to the shape of the floor.

"Where—?"

"We're in the cellar at the shop," Archie said.

I raised my hands to my face, taking a little inventory, noting that some kind of gash at my right temple seemed to be the cause of the blood. I groaned, rolled over, pushed myself into a sitting position. Kept my eyes closed, head in hands, against the vertigo. In a moment I felt like I could open them.

Archie knelt beside me, clearly having no clue what to do.

He looked a little gray in the face but otherwise unharmed. I imagined his wan expression came from looking at me.

"What happened?" I asked.

He looked a little discomfited. "Gabrielle pushed you."

I remembered. "We were in the shop."

"Yes. You fell down the steps."

And you really came to my rescue there, didn't you, he-man? I didn't say it. I shifted my weight a little. My lower back hurt like hell. Breathing was agony around my ribcage. I could see where my jeans were ripped across one knee, and the left sleeve of my blazer was barely hanging by a few threads. I looked over toward the stone steps leading up to the shop. It was a wonder Gabrielle hadn't killed me.

"Give me a hand," I said.

I worked to get my legs under me. Archie helped pull me to my feet. A blade of pain ripped through my left hip when I put my weight on it.

"Where is she now?" I asked.

He pulled a handkerchief from his pocket and wiped at a tiny smear of blood on his hand.

"She's gone. Said she was getting something ready and she would be back soon."

I limped over to a chest of drawers that the movers hadn't taken away yet and leaned on it for support.

"Archie, what the hell is going on here? Why did Gabrielle come after me?"

But my question fell on deaf ears. He'd already crossed to the far wall and turned to pace the distance again.

"I'm so worried for Catherine," he said.

"Catherine?"

"Gabrielle just seems so very determined."

I didn't know what strange little games this bunch were playing but I knew I wanted out of there. Now. I looked toward the stairs, calculating whether I could possibly climb them.

"It's no use," Archie said, guessing my thoughts. "She's locked it from the other side."

"You don't have a key?"

"She took them."

Once again, I cursed his passivity. How could he sit back and just let himself become a victim? Let alone stand for what Gabrielle had done to me. I glanced at my watch but it was smashed. Surely Louisa would get worried when I didn't come home and she would come to check on me.

And find what? There was no way she could know we were in the cellar. At least she might contact the police and tell them I was missing. I clung to that hope.

"Is there an opening from the street down to this cellar?" I asked Archie. "You know the type, where businesses receive deliveries?"

I knew the answer to that almost as soon as I'd phrased the question. Louisa and I had spent the night down here and examined every nook and cranny for traces of the unexplained haunting. There was no delivery chute.

"What time is it?" I asked.

Archie pushed up the sleeve of his cardigan but his arm was bare. "I guess I left my watch in the apartment."

Well, fine. I was back to hoping that enough time had gone by for Louisa to get worried about me. I tested my legs to see if I could walk. Each step sent a jolt through my left leg and each breath was agony. I could probably get up the stairs in a life-or-death move but it would be foolish to waste the energy to go up there to find that the door was locked, and then have to make the painful journey back down. I needed to think this out before I exhausted my small reserve of energy.

"Have you checked the door?" I asked. "Maybe she closed it but forgot to lock it?"

He shook his head. "It's locked."

"Is my purse down here?"

Archie turned his head, glancing around.

"Can you look for it? I might have something in there that could help us."

He moved around the room, finally spotting it beside the steps. He picked it up in that uneasy way that most men carry a woman's purse and brought it to me.

I spied a chair in the corner. I wasn't at all sure I could get back up from its overstuffed depths once I sat, but standing around wasn't helping my hip at all either. Limping over to it, I sank down into the cushion and allowed myself to simply melt. It was the only scrap of comfort I'd felt yet.

My bag sported a few new scuffs and when I unzipped the top I was greeted by the heavenly scent of the bottle of eucalyptus lotion I carried with me. The plastic cap had split and nearly everything in the purse wore a coat of it. Would this night just keep getting better and better? I scraped enough of the silky stuff off my small bottle of ibuprofen to get it open and wiped the spare lotion into my skin. Tapped four of the little brown pills into the palm of my hand.

"Is there any water down here?" My luck, it would be a bottle that one of the sweaty movers had left behind but I could hardly afford to be picky.

Archie dithered around some more but didn't come up with anything. I worked up as much spit as I could and worked the pills down. A dozen swallows or so and they felt like they might actually make it to my stomach.

While hoping for some result from the pain meds I continued my trek through the purse. One of Dolly's knitted afghans lay over the back of my chair and I used it to wipe lotion off each item that I pulled from the purse. I wanted to feel badly about messing up her handiwork but I was at that screw-it-all point in the evening where my own comfort was selfishly taking precedence over everything else.

I tried to remember what the doorknob at the top of the stairs looked like. When I'd been here with Louisa we'd just left the door standing open. As near as I could remember it was secured with a rather old-fashioned lock that might easily be circumvented with a piece of plastic. I pulled a credit card that I rarely use out of my wallet and handed it to Archie.

"Go up there and see if this will work," I told him.

He gave it a blank look and I explained in detail how to do it. What planet had this man grown up on?

"Sorry. I didn't have much call for this skill as manager of a sales team," he said as he trudged up the steps.

I heard a lot of fiddling around and a few grunts. No reassuring squeak of the door coming open.

"It's the other lock that seems to be the sticking point," he said, coming back down and handing me the card.

"There's a deadbolt on it?" I hadn't remembered that part.

"Well, yes, apparently so."

Sheesh. I gritted my teeth and resumed the search

through the purse. If only I'd thought to pack my hammer and chisel we could tried digging our way out through that old bricked-up doorway into the tunnels. And end up god knows where. A better use would be to remove the hinges from the door, but without the tools that wasn't happening either.

Archie continued to stand there and watch me rummage.

"You might check around and see if there is anything in this cellar in the way of tools," I suggested. "Maybe the movers left a hammer or something behind." Did a girl have to think of *everything* around here?

"Oh, here's something that might do the trick," he called out after a few minutes. He held up a pair of office scissors.

I wanted to cry when he handed them to me. How on earth were those going to open a locked door? I set them beside me and continued to pull things from the purse—besides wallet and pill bottle, I came up with my ring of keys from home which I sent Archie up the stairs again to try. By some miracle one of them might work. But no such luck on that.

Other than that it seemed we were reduced to using a hairbrush, a lip balm, a ballpoint pen or my small spiral notebook. I was just about to consider how the pen and metal coil from the notebook might be disassembled into lock picking tools when I heard a sound from above.

A second later the door opened. Gabrielle was back.

Chapter 26

She closed the door behind her and came lightly down the stairs. "Almost ready, darling," she said. "I've been to the market for food, and I've collected my things from home. By tomorrow night, we'll be in a posh hotel room in Paris."

Her eyes were on Archie the whole time she was outlining her plan. Then she noticed that I was up. Her face hardened.

I tried to imagine what I must look like. Blood from the cut beside my eye had probably dried in a trickle all the way down to my chin. My hair must be tangled and full of floor grime and dust balls. Same for my clothing, with rips and tears added.

"What'll we do with her?" Gabrielle said to Archie.

He gave her a blank stare.

C'mon Arch, speak up for me, I begged silently. But he didn't.

"You can just leave me here," I said.

Gabrielle didn't seem to notice that I'd spoken. I debated launching myself out of the chair but knew that she would move a lot quicker than I possibly could right now.

"Well, no matter. I've got only one more little errand, my love, and then we're off," she said, her smile back in place. She pointed toward the ceiling. "I'll just pack a little bag for you. Your passport's upstairs?"

Without waiting for a response, she whirled around and rushed up the stairs.

"Catch her!" I hissed at Archie. "Hold the door open!"

But he didn't react quickly enough and we heard the deadbolt snap firmly shut.

I jammed all my stuff back into my battered purse and edged my way forward on the chair seat, hoping my legs would hold me a bit better now that the pain was subsiding.

"What's going on here, Archie?" I demanded. "You're planning to run off now with Gabrielle? What about Catherine?"

I hobbled toward him and faced him down.

"What about it!"

His pallid skin faded another two shades. "I—I . . . I don't know. I never planned this."

"Well, Gabrielle seems to think the two of you are going off together, toward some happy life in Paris. Where did she get that idea if you didn't have a hand in the plans?"

Upstairs, I heard muffled sounds. Archie rolled his eyes up toward them.

"Archie! Explanation!"

He crumpled. His shoulders slumped and he backed into a straight upright chair. "I never thought she would . . ."

I stood in front of him. "Start at the beginning."

"I'd hoped to make Dolly give up the idea of this silly shop. I wanted back in our home, be with our friends at the club. I figured if we were back there, close to our old lifestyle, I might get my job back or at least have the contacts among the country club set to get another good position."

"And to stay close to Catherine?"

"Well, yes, right."

"But Dolly knew about the long-term affair between the two of you and she did all she could to keep you here in town. Not that it made much sense to locate her shop in this building, which Catherine Devon owns."

"That was the one suggestion of mine that Dolly actually accepted. The location is top-notch and the rent was reasonable. It's not as if Catherine were in the building much time at all anyway."

"And the pranks started as a way to get Dolly to reconsider moving back to your old house? Were you behind all of them?"

"Only a few. I accidentally made the muddy footprints the first time. Slipped off my shoes and stowed them away. When Dolly became so upset, it gave me the idea that she might be convinced, with a little persuasion, that the place was haunted. From time to time I made noises in the night. Whenever she took her sleeping pills I could sneak downstairs and spray some perfume or make footprints. Back in the bedroom I would pretend I'd been awakened by a noise and she would insist that we both go downstairs to investigate. Once I released a tiny smoke bomb and she became convinced it was an apparition."

"You probably fed her a lot of stories of the haunted places around town, adding a little fuel to the fire or something?"

He nodded. "But I never did anything to cause her harm. I swear it."

"You didn't switch the tea cups when she scalded her hand?"

"No—absolutely not." He looked up at me.

I pulled another of the straight chairs over and sat gingerly on it. "How does Gabrielle fit into all this?"

"I began to suspect her of some of the nastier pranks after one time when she and I . . . um . . ."

"Were you also sleeping with *her*?" My incredulity began to climb.

"She began to come on to me, right after she started working here," he said. "Young woman, older man. I know I should have fended her off, but that sort of thing can appeal to a man's self-confidence, you know. By that time Dolly had ended the physical side of our relationship." He squirmed as he said it. "And I was rarely able to get out and see Catherine. But I swear it was mostly a matter of a few stolen kisses in moments when no one was around."

I watched his face for signs of deception, certain that he was still hiding something.

"There was just the once," he said. "Down here in the cellar one evening when Dolly went to a card game with her friends. Gabrielle had worked late and she asked me to carry something down for her. When I turned around she was right behind me. Threw herself at me, she did. I . . . well, we ended up on the leather sofa that was here."

Gabrielle had given that sofa a loving stroke with her hand as the movers carried it out. Maybe that small motion brought it home to her that Archie would soon be going away. With someone else.

I glanced around the cellar. The night Louisa and I had stayed here I'd taken a short nap on that same sofa. And I'd had a vivid dream about Drake and myself. I blushed. Maybe suggestive scents on the leather or within the fibers of the woven blanket had exerted an effect on me. Ew. I forced myself to follow a different line of thinking.

"So, when did Gabrielle reveal this plan to you—the idea of running off together?"

"I swear, it was never a plan. Not the way you're thinking. She's cooked up the whole thing herself."

I mulled it over. Archie, for all the deceptions he pulled with his wife, had seemed genuinely concerned when Dolly died. And his surprise at Gabrielle's recent actions felt authentic to me. Maybe the clues to the younger woman's state of mind had been there all along.

"I don't know . . . I truly don't know . . ." Archie murmured, his head in his hands.

Upstairs, the few sounds had stopped I realized with a start. How much time had gone by? Much longer than Gabrielle needed to grab a few clothes for Archie. I gazed again at my watch for several seconds, forgetting that its shattered face wasn't going to tell me anything.

"I can't go with her," he said. "Do you think she'll understand that?"

I didn't see Gabrielle being very sympathetic toward what she would perceive as a change of heart on his part.

The girl was obviously thinking that her romantic crush on Archie was reciprocated. She seemed quite firm in her plans.

"I don't hear anything upstairs, do you?" I asked, trying to bring myself back to more practical matters—like how on earth we would get out of here.

Archie raised his head and cocked an ear toward the door.

"Can you go up there and check?"

He came back down in less than a minute. "I don't hear a thing."

"What was it she said before she left—that she had one more small errand to do? Any idea what that might be?"

He shook his head slowly. He might have been successful in the business world but I swear that I've never met a man more clueless about women. I'd felt sorry for him, being pushed around by his wife all those years, but I was beginning to see her side of it. If anything was to happen, someone needed to take charge and Archie was clearly not doing it.

Edging forward in my chair again, I decided I better test my own limits, find out how much I might be capable of when the moment of truth arrived. I stood and took a few steps. The sharp jabs earlier had eased into a dull overall ache now. Except for my ribs. The first deep breath almost brought me to my knees.

"I'm going back to the softer chair," I said. "Tell me if you hear any sounds from the shop. Anything at all. If someone other than Gabrielle should show up we need to bang on the door and shout for help."

He dutifully climbed to the small landing and stood

there with his ear to the door. I used baby steps and an old-woman's groan to get me into the depths of the armchair. I tried to calculate how long we'd been down here, but with no idea how long I'd lain unconscious on the floor there wasn't much way to know.

Plus, what did it matter? We were here now.

I rested my head against the back of the chair, trying to focus on plots for escape and rescue. At some point I dozed. I know this because I woke myself with a buzz-saw snore. A trickle of saliva trailed out of the corner of my mouth and I wiped at it with the grimy sleeve of my blazer.

Archie had given up his post at the door and come back down to find a warmer surface than the stone steps. He sat on the edge of a console table, picking at his cuticles.

I stood up too fast. My head swam and every single one of my aches and bruises screamed at me. The ibuprofen's effects had worn off, which meant it had been at least four hours since Gabrielle left. What type of 'quick' errand could she possibly be doing? What if she'd had a traffic accident or been picked up by the police, or simply headed off to France without Archie? We might be down here for a hundred years before someone found our skeletons with scary, toothy grins.

Stop it, Charlie. Right this instant.

For one thing, at least one person had to be looking for me—Louisa. And Catherine would start wondering where Archie was. She had a key to the building. Surely someone would come along.

As if by divine response, I heard a small noise upstairs. I sucked in my breath. Ouch. Slowly breathed out again.

The doorknob rattled, but of course it was Gabrielle.

"All done," she announced gaily. She practically skipped down the stairs and put an arm around Archie. "We're ready to go."

"I'm not going with you, Gabrielle," he said quietly.

"Of course you are. It's all planned."

He shook his head.

"Darling, all the obstacles are out of the way now. We're free. I've taken care of all of them."

"Them?" I said. "Gabrielle, what have you done?"

She gave me a glare that made me wish I'd just stayed quietly in my corner until they'd gone.

She turned back to Archie. "The car is packed, darling. A few hours to the coast, through the Chunnel, and we'll be ready to start our new life."

He shook his head again. She slapped him.

"We *are* going! We have plans. We'll have a life together. With all of Dolly's money." Her overly-sweet tone had gone rigid and hard. "You told me I was the love of your life."

"I never—" His mouth hung open.

"I got rid of that possessive wife of yours for you. When we couldn't scare her off, I gave her the pills. And now I've taken care of the other one too."

"Catherine? You've hurt Catherine?" Pain contorted his face.

Gabrielle's eyes sparked with fire. "It's the two of us now, Archie. You'll not reject *me*."

She spun toward me. "What trash have you been telling him?" Her words came out through clenched teeth.

"I've not told him anything, Gabrielle. This is crazy. Just let me go and the two of you can do whatever you want."

"Oh, and have you running right to the police? No bloody way!"

What did that mean? Did she plan to get rid of everyone who knew what she'd done?

"Come, Archie. We'll go quietly, leave the place locked up. No one will ever know she's down here."

My mind raced through the possibilities but if Catherine truly was gone that didn't leave anyone who could get into the cellar. I really would become a stack of dried out old bones.

I tried to send visual signals to Archie—get out, call for help, jam the door so she can't lock it—anything. But he was speaking quietly, trying to reason with her and make everyone play nice again.

I pushed past the pain to rush her, thinking maybe I could reach the top of the stairs first. But she elbowed my ribs the moment I got within striking distance, and that took the breath out of me.

"Get over there," she said, shoving me backward into the armchair.

"Gabrielle, listen to me," Archie said. "Please don't do it this way. Please listen to reason."

But she was way beyond reason. She grabbed up a heavy silver bookend and advanced on me. I wanted to melt into the chair's depths. I gripped the edges of the seat cushion and my fingers closed around something hard and cold. The scissors.

Chapter 27

Her face contorted in anger, her eyes went wild. I kept my eyes on the hand with the bookend while I tightened my grip on the scissors and tried to think what to do with them. Stab or slice? I didn't want to do either but I wasn't about to let her clock me in the head with that thing.

Movement behind Gabrielle caught my eye. She swung the bookend at me just as Archie reached around her from behind. He tried to pin her arms at her sides, but she saw him at the last millisecond and turned on him. The momentum sent the heavy silver object right toward his face.

I jumped up, stumbling when the hip pain hit me, my scissor-weapon still in hand. Archie had wrestled Gabrielle to the floor and she'd dropped the silver bookend, just beyond his grasp. I didn't wait to find out how it would all end. I scrambled for the stairs, wincing with each footfall, holding my breath tightly against the pain in my ribs.

At the top I dared a glance back. Archie had kicked the bookend farther beyond the fray. Gabrielle was trying to punch at him with her fists but he'd grabbed both her wrists. I leaned against the door, half tempted to lock them both inside, but afraid of how that might end up. At the moment, my bigger concern was getting air into my lungs.

I managed two shallow breaths before I realized that I was hearing a noise from the front of the shop. Someone was pounding on the window. I hobbled to the doorway and almost cried out in relief.

It was Louisa. And at the shop's door, two policemen in nice solid black uniforms stood with nightsticks in hand. I limped toward the door and let them in.

"The cellar—" My breath caught. The ribs were killing me. "Gabrielle—the woman down there. She murdered—"

Luckily, they didn't want more from me at that moment. They headed toward the dim light showing from the stairwell.

Louisa rushed toward me.

"Don't hug—" I pointed to my ribs.

"Oh, baby. You're a mess."

I nodded.

She whipped out her cell phone and called for an ambulance.

"I was so worried," she said. "You didn't come after an hour, then it was two hours. I called the police but they tried to convince me you'd just gone out for some fun. It took me forever to persuade them that wasn't the case."

I looked around for a place to sit but the empty shop offered nothing. I leaned against the wall. Voices came from the cellar—shouts, followed by a shriek and noises of a struggle.

"They searched the park and the graveyard. I tried calling the shop, since you'd told me you were coming here, but the phone's disconnected. I came by but everything was dark."

I nodded. "I had a feeling . . ."

"Don't try to talk. They'll be here soon."

"It's morning!" I'd only now realized that the street outside was in daylight and a few cars had passed in front of the shop.

Louisa nodded. The unusual sound of a foreign ambulance siren came closer.

From below, the male voices grew louder as they approached the top of the steps. One of the police officers had a grip on Gabrielle's elbow. Her hands were in cuffs behind her back. Her perky hair clip was askew and blond chunks spiked out at all angles. The pale pink sweater and print skirt she'd worn for her going-away trip with Archie were dingy with floor grime, the skirt hanging lopsidedly from a rip near the waistband. She sent me a hard stare before lowering her gaze to the ground as the officer led her outside.

Archie's clothing was equally grimy and he was holding a handkerchief to a scrape near his hairline. The second officer followed. I wondered what was going through his mind.

"Sorry about all this," Archie said to me. "Quite th—"

"What about Catherine?" I interrupted.

"Oh lord." Archie turned to the policeman behind him and started to explain.

The ambulance dodged its way around the moving van that still sat there, found a spot in front of it, almost at the curb. Two uniformed EMTs jumped out and dashed to the back for a stretcher.

"I'm all right," I tried to insist. But it became clear that I really should have everything checked out when I tried to walk across the room and nearly fell. Louisa and the policeman each took an elbow and the paramedics insisted that I sit on the edge of the stretcher while they did quick checks of my blood pressure and heart rate and took a peek at the wound on my temple.

I wanted to argue that I could easily ride to the hospital sitting up, but suddenly the soft cushion on the gurney looked really good. I laid down and just gave control over to everyone else, for once.

* * *

It was mid-afternoon when Louisa took me back to her house. By this time of day we were supposed to have been arriving in London, settling into our hotel and dressing for dinner and a play. A bunch of strapping around my ribs and a sizeable dosing of pain killers had me feeling good enough that I was actually up for it, but Louisa's more sensible argument prevailed and I was put to bed with chicken soup and a pile of thick blankets.

The very proper British doctor had suggested, in his *very* polite way, that I not travel for a week or so. I had no intention of minding that order.

"If we go to sleep now, we can set our alarms for two a.m.," I told Louisa. "I'll easily make my flight and you'll have me out of your hair."

"I don't want you out of my hair, darling," she said

as she tucked the covers around me. "Stay as long as you like."

But I could tell that the past day's adventure had worn on her a bit too much as well. When I reached for my bedside clock and set it, she shook her head good-naturedly and went to do the same.

My body nestled into the cushiony surface of the mattress and I must have been asleep within minutes. At some point in my sleep I heard the distant sound of a telephone ringing but it could have been a dream. I shifted my position slightly, without ever opening my eyes.

Light tapping, a swish of door against carpet, and Louisa's voice whispered, "Charlie?"

I smiled under painkiller influence and opened one eye.

"Are you awake? Telephone for you."

Drake. I'd intended to let him know that everything was on schedule for my flight. But it wasn't my hubby. Archie Jones greeted me.

"Charlie, I wanted to say how sorry I am about your injuries. I'd no idea that Gabrielle would take this thing so far."

"What's happened? Is she being held by the police?" A scary flash went through my head, of Gabrielle on the loose and trying to finish what she'd started.

"Oh, yes. She'll not be out for a long time," he said. "Mainly I wanted to thank you for your efforts, and to say that Catherine is all right."

While I'd been babying my scrapes and cracked ribs, I'd completely forgotten that Gabrielle had gone after Catherine with the intention of 'fixing' her.

"Gabrielle apparently went to Catherine's home but was

refused entry by a maid. The police said she then broke into the garages and tampered with something on Catherine's car, but she left enough traces of the handiwork that Catherine became suspicious and had the vehicle towed and checked before getting behind the wheel. The police took some prints or swabs or whatever it is they do."

"I'm glad. Hopefully they got enough evidence to make a strong case."

"Well, that's the other thing. Now it seems that Gabrielle has recanted the confessions she made to us and the case will definitely go to trial."

"Will I need to come back to testify?" At this very moment the prospect didn't sound at all appealing.

"My solicitor believes that my testimony will be sufficient," he said. "I'm sure they will let you know."

I nodded and mumbled something. He thanked me again for helping to solve the mystery of the phantom pranks and for getting Gabrielle out of his life. I was dimly aware that Louisa plucked the portable phone from my fingers, but sleep rapidly overtook me.

Bless her heart, my aunt continued to watch out for me—packing my bag and carrying it downstairs, making the middle-of-night drive without a blink while I filled her in on the strangeness of the previous night. A gingerly hug in consideration of my tender ribs, and an invitation to come back, with the sincere desire that we never let go of our newfound relationship.

"I'll miss you, darling girl," she said. "I hope this whole escapade hasn't put you off England forever."

"Absolutely not. I loved Bury and I will definitely find a chance to come back." I noticed that her blue eyes seemed a little moist. "Louisa, it's been a wonderful adventure and I wouldn't have given up the time with you for anything."

She gave my hand a squeeze and then saw me through airport check-in and made sure an attendant with a wheelchair would take me to the plane. It wasn't the first time I'd ever boarded a plane in wounded condition, but I chafed a little at all the fuss.

More of the pain pills, my business class seat fully reclined, and I have to admit that Dallas came along more quickly than I would have imagined. During the layover for the quick hop to Albuquerque I called Drake. Hearing that I was now west of the Mississippi gave both of us a sense of reassurance. I guess you have to live in the West to really know the feeling.

"My job is ending tonight," he said. "I'll be home tomorrow." He sounded excited that more Alaska work for the summer looked like a sure bet. "I left the business card for the boarding kennel on the dining table. I hate to admit how much I've missed that little pup. Have Freckles home with you when I get there?"

I agreed. I also didn't go into detail about my last twenty-four hours; there would be time enough for him to learn about it once we were all home. Safe and sound.

Author's Notes

The first seed of the idea for this book came during a trip to Bury St. Edmunds, where the people are so friendly and the history just a little mind-boggling to an American like me. The Angel Hotel is an amazing place to stay. I have my daughter to thank for letting me tag along and for introducing me to the lovely people she works with in Bury.

Readers familiar with the location will recognize some real sites: The Angel Hotel, the sugar factory, Abbeygate Street and of course the Abbey ruins, gardens and cathedral. Certain actual businesses are used, but the ones central to the story—the Trahorn Building, The Knit and Purl, and several others—are purely fictional. All the events in the story are fictional. The police station, newspaper office, museum and other real places have been altered by my pen to serve the purposes of this fictional story. I do not know if Louisa's haunted sites tours exist—if so, they probably do not resemble the one I made up for this story—but the ghosts mentioned by name do come from local lore and most certainly do exist, for those who believe.

As always I am thankful for my husband Dan who has stuck with all the ups and downs of my writing career, through eighteen books over the last twenty-two years. My longtime friend and editor, Susan Slater, is there for my impossible deadlines and always comes through in a pinch. My dear friend Margaret Norrie was very kind in reading the early manuscript and giving me the British perspective on the characters and story. My everlasting thanks to her for pointing out the things that an English person would never do—I saved those bits for my uncouth American characters.

And of course there are my readers, many of whom take the time to send me encouraging notes and to so considerately spread the word by recommending my books to their friends. My heartfelt thanks to all of you!

Connie Shelton
May, 2012

Books
by Connie Shelton

THE CHARLIE PARKER SERIES

Deadly Gamble
Vacations Can Be Murder
Partnerships Can Be Murder
Small Towns Can Be Murder
Memories Can Be Murder
Honeymoons Can Be Murder
Reunions Can Be Murder
Competition Can Be Murder
Balloons Can Be Murder
Obsessions Can Be Murder
Gossip Can Be Murder
Stardom Can Be Murder
Phantoms Can Be Murder

Holidays Can Be Murder - a Christmas novella

THE SAMANTHA SWEET SERIES

Sweet Masterpiece
Sweet's Sweets
Sweet Holidays
Sweet Hearts

More Charlie!

What's next in store for Charlie and Drake? Another
mystery back home in Albuquerque, or will they be off
to fly helicopters in Alaska?
Watch for the next Charlie Parker book in 2013!

And . . . Connie is pleased to announce a new mystery
series, featuring Samantha Sweet.
Sam breaks into houses for a living.
But she's really a baker with a magical touch, who
invites you to her delightful pastry shop—
Sweet's Sweets.
Don't miss this new series!

Sign up for Connie's free email mystery newsletter and
get announcements of new books, discount coupons, and
the chance for some 'sweet' deals.

connieshelton.com

**Contact by email: connie@connieshelton.com
Follow Connie Shelton on Twitter, Pinterest
and Facebook**

CPSIA information can be obtained at www.ICGtesting.com
Printed in the USA
LVOW11s1930261113

362983LV00011B/201/P